"WHAT HAVE YOU BEEN
WAITING FOR, LONGARM,
AN ENGRAVED INVITATION?"

"I just waited long enough to make sure," Longarm told Mae. He brought up his hands and cupped them around her generous breasts, slightly pendulous now that she was leaning forward. As he began caressing them he added, "And you were so busy—"

"I'm not that busy now." Mae wrung out the sleeve and let it fall. Her hands worked for a quick moment at the buttons on the side placket of her skirt, then she pulled her camisole out of the skirt and pushed the skirt down to her thighs. "And I don't want to wait any longer..."

Also in the **LONGARM** series
from Jove

TABOR EVANS

LONGARM
AND THE
SNAKE DANCERS

A JOVE BOOK

LONGARM AND THE SNAKE DANCERS

A Jove Book / published by arrangement with
the author

PRINTING HISTORY
Jove edition / January 1983

ISBN: 0-515-06252-9

Chapter 1

Longarm took out one of his long thin cheroots as he stepped onto the observation platform of the last coach on the westbound Santa Fe flyer. The train had gained very little speed on the gentle drag upslope from the Gallup depot, but it suddenly seemed to speed up and the thrumming of the wheels on the rails took on a hollow, echoing timbre. Longarm delayed lighting his cheroot to look for and identify the reason for the change.

A quick glance gave him the answer. The train had topped the ten miles of rising ground that had slowed its progress when it pulled out of Gallup and was now crossing a long trestle that raised the ties and rails above the flood level of a huge dry wash. The trestle bisected the shallow, sagebrush-dotted floor of an oblong basin shaped like the bowl of a spoon. The long dimension of the basin lay east and west, and its sides stretched from a massive sandstone hump on the north to a ragged, gravel-studded vertical edge half a dozen miles to the south.

His eyes narrowing against the harsh, beating glare of the early afternoon sun, Longarm studied the towering chunk of ocher sandstone. Halfway up its sheer side that towered three or four hundred feet above the rails, he saw an oval recess, like a bubble cut in half, that broke the solid face of the formation. The size of the great stone hump and its distance from the train gave it a false scale. Holding unlighted the match he'd pulled from his vest pocket, Longarm gazed at the cliff for a long moment before he realized

1

that the rectangular, blocklike shapes visible inside the recess were houses.

Now, that's one hell of a place to build a house, old son, he told himself as he flicked the tip of the wooden match across the iron-hard edge of his thumbnail. The match sputtered into life and he cupped it in his hands while he waited for the first sulfurous fumes to dissipate before lighting the cherott. *A man would really have some stairs to climb when he came home for supper, if he lived in a place like that.*

Ahead, the locomotive whistle wailed sadly. Longarm leaned around the edge of the coach and peered ahead along the tracks. More high ground lay ahead. The engine had left the trestle now and was climbing through a cut in a high sandstone ledge, and beyond the first ledge the raw, ragged rims of others rose against the pale blue sky. As the train began to lose speed on the progressively steeper grade, Longarm puffed the cheroot and watched the smoke twirl away from him in a thin gray trail.

The train left the trestle and entered a steep, narrow cut, and the wind whisked a cloud of sooty coal smoke around the end of the coach. Longarm soon tired of seeing nothing on either side except the tan faces of boulders outlined in thin streaks of soil only a little darker than the stone. Tossing away the stub of his cheroot, he went back into the coach.

He paid little attention to the half-dozen other passengers. He'd scanned all the faces of the riders in this car as well as the two ahead, but had seen nobody matching the descriptions on the "Wanted" lists that kept piling up in the U. S. Marshal's Denver office.

In his seat again, Longarm leaned back and pulled the wide brim of his tobacco-brown Stetson down to shade his gunmetal-blue eyes and closed them. He had just begun to doze when the screech of steel brakes on steel wheels broke the lazy rhythm that was lulling him to sleep. The coach rattled and buckled as the train jerked for several moments, then groaned to a sudden halt.

The passengers began opening windows and leaning out, peering toward the front of the train. One or two of the men stood up and poked their shoulders out of the windows beside their seats to get a better view.

2

Longarm stood up, too, but he didn't bother looking out the window. A sudden stop in this kind of country could mean trouble of several kinds. Striding to the front vestibule, Longarm wrenched the door open and dropped to the ground. Settling his gunbelt more firmly on his hips, he started toward the front of the train.

Even before he'd passed the baggage coach, with only the tender and the engine ahead, Longarm could see the reason for the train's emergency stop. One wall of the man-made cut through which the rails ran had given way. A boulder as big as a house had rolled across the rails, blocking the cut completely. On top of the huge stone and along the short stretch of track between it and the engine, other smaller boulders lay scattered where they'd rolled after the wall of the cut collapsed.

Longarm walked up to the engineer and conductor, who stood in the narrow space between the locomotive and the walls of the cut. In front of them there were a half-dozen curious passengers who'd also alighted when the train stopped.

"And it was damn lucky we were on this straight stretch of track," the engineer was saying. "I just got the string stopped before we hit the first of them boulders."

"You braked in time, and I guess that's all that matters," the conductor told him. "But we're sure not going to get through that slide for a while."

"How long are we going to have to lay over?" one of the passengers asked.

"I can't even guess yet," the conductor replied. "I'll know a little more after I scrabble over those rocks and see how much rail the slide took out. But we won't be moving in a hurry. It's going to take a while for a work train to get here and clear the right-of-way."

Longarm had worked his way through the gathering crowd of passengers by now. The conductor's name was Bob Grey, he remembered. The trainman had introduced himself when he'd punched Longarm's government travel voucher the day before, in Raton, and they'd exchanged a few casual words during the long miles as the train rolled south to Albuquerque and then jogged west toward Gallup.

3

"Anything I can do, Bob?" Longarm asked.

"Oh, Marshal Long," Grey said. "No, I don't think there's much the law can do about something like this. It's a railroad job."

"If you need a hand, just let me know," Longarm offered.

"Well, now—" The conductor hesitated for a moment, then said, "I'll have to send one brakeman back to flag, and I ought to leave one with the train. Jim and his tallow pot are going to have to stay with the loco, too, so if you feel like climbing over that slide with me—"

"Sure. Whatever you say," Longarm nodded.

"Soon as I start a flagman back down the right-of-way, I'll hook up my key and notify division at Albuquerque," Grey went on, as much to himself as to Longarm. "Then we'll crawl over the slide and see how bad it is, and I'll pick up the wire on the other side and notify the Kingman division to sidetrack whatever trains are rolling east."

Picking their way over the loose, shifting rocks and boulders that were spread across the tracks for a distance of more than a quarter of a mile, Longarm and Bob Grey traversed the slide. At the end of the jumble of stone and loose earth, the conductor pointed to a truncated slanting pole from which the railroad telegraph wire dangled in loose coils.

"I'll hook up and tell the division office at Kingman what's happened here, and we can go on back," he said, taking his telegraph key from his coat pocket.

Their brief walk from the train had brought them to the crest of the spur of the Chuska Mountains that marked the western boundary of New Mexico Territory. Below them the arid land stretched endlessly in undulating ripples. Through the thin clear air Longarm could see the broken line of the San Francisco Peaks that rose at the southern end of the Coconino Plateau, and in all that vast expanse no living thing moved.

"Arizona Territory's a real lonesome place," he remarked to Grey as the trainman came back, pocketing his telegraph key.

"Yes, it is," the conductor agreed. He gestured that they could start back to the train, and as they picked their way

4

slowly over the piled slide, went on, "The Santa Fe's brought a few people in, though, and there'll be more. When I first got on this run, all there was to Winslow and Holbrook was a few shacks left when the railheads moved on west. Now they've both grown up into pretty good towns. But I guess you've been this way before, haven't you, Marshal Long?"

"That'd depend on what you call this way. A while back I had a case down at Yuma, and before that I was in the Gila River country, and up at the Four Corners. Seems like the cases that've brought me to Arizona Territory has been further north or south."

"If I remember, it's Winslow your travel voucher called for. I hope you're not in a hurry to get there."

"Not especially, Bob. Even when I do, I'll just stop long enough to start up north, to the Navajo Reservation."

"Trouble up there that the Indian Bureau can't handle?"

"Well, now, I'm in about the same fix you was back there right after the train stopped. I won't know much till I get to Winslow and find out just what is wrong."

"If you're going up into Navajo country, there's a lady passenger on this run you might like to talk to. I know her because she makes a lot of trips between Winslow and Albuqerque."

"I never pass up a chance to meet a pretty lady, Bob, but what gives you the idea I want to get acquainted with this one?"

"Why, she's got a trading post up in the north part of the Navajo Reservation," Grey explained. "I'd imagine she could tell you something about the country there."

Longarm nodded. "It might be a good idea, at that."

"I'll introduce you to her when we get back to the train," the conductor promised. "Her name's Mrs. Blaisdell, and you'll have plenty of time to talk to her. Before I got off the wire when I was reporting to Albuquerque the brass-pounder there passed on word from the division super that the Santa Fe's going to pay for your rooms and meals at the Harvey House in Gallup until the slide's cleared."

"You got any idea how long we'll be held up?"

"Just guessing, but I'd say by this time tomorrow we'll

be rolling again. It's not a real bad job. The work train from Albuquerque ought to be here by sundown, and they'll work all night and right on through tomorrow until they've got the right-of-way cleared."

By the time Longarm and Grey reached the train, most of the passengers had gotten off and were strolling somewhat aimlessly around in the restricted space between the coaches and the walls of the cut. After having a word with the engineer, Grey motioned to Longarm.

"We'll go find Mrs. Blaisdell now, if you're still of a mind to talk to her," he said. "As soon as we get up steam again, we'll start backing down the grade to Gallup, and I'm going to be busy telling the passengers that the Santa Fe's going to pay their bills at the Harvey House until we can move on again."

"That's fine with me," Longarm nodded. "You lead the way."

Threading their way through the shifting knots of passengers, the two men moved to the end of the coaches and part of the way up the opposite side of the train.

Grey stopped and pointed. "That's Mrs. Blaisdell, there by that big boulder halfway to the side of the cut."

Longarm studied the woman they were approaching. He recalled having noticed her when she boarded the train at Albuquerque, because it was unusual to see a woman travelling alone. He'd paid little attention to her then; he'd been looking for faces that matched descriptions on the "Wanted" flyers, and no women were being sought by the Federal government at that particular time.

Mae Blaisdell wore a split riding skirt, cut short in the Western style. The hem of the brown covert-cloth garment barely reached to her calves, where it brushed the tops of her soft leather low-heeled boots. Her hands were thrust into the side pockets of a matching jacket; though it was sleeveless, the jacket was too long to be called a vest. It bulged over her high full breasts, was pinched in at the waist by a silver-trimmed belt, then dropped to just below her hips. Under the jacket she had on a long-sleeved linen blouse with a high ruffled neckline.

6

Her face was shaded by the wide brim of the cavalry campaign hat she had on, which had four side creases that drew its crown into a low Montana-style peak. As they drew closer and her features became clear in the shade of the hat-brim, Longarm saw that she was not as young as her generous high-breasted figure at first suggested. At close range, he could see tiny wrinkles at the corners of her eyes and the beginning of a pair of bracket lines at the sides of her full red lips.

Her face was slightly tanned, her nose slightly uptilted, her eyes light blue. When she spoke to the conductor, her voice had the slight edge of one who spends a lot of time outdoors in wide country where a shout is used more often than a normal conversational voice.

"Well, how long are we going to have to wait, Bob?" she asked.

"Till sometime tomorrow," Grey replied. "But don't get upset, Mae. The Santa Fe's paying for your rooms and meals at the Harvey House in Gallup until the track's clear."

"That's fine," she replied, "but it's not going to make up for Hosteen Clau having to be away from the post a day longer than he'd expected, and it's not going to make up for me losing a day, either."

"We're all sorry, Mae, but it can't be helped," the trainman replied. "Matter of fact, you ought to count yourself lucky that it happened here, where we can back up to Gallup pretty quick."

"I suppose you're right."

Grey went on, "The reason I was looking for you is to introduce you to Marshal Long."

Longarm touched his hat. "Right pleased to meet you, Mrs. Blaisdell."

"Thank you, Marshal. The pleasure's mutual, I'm sure."

"Marshal Long works out of Denver," Grey said. "He's here to—well, I guess he can tell you that better than I can. Anyhow, he'll be up in your part of Navajo country sooner or later, so I thought you two might start getting acquainted now."

Longarm said quickly, "Seeing as how I'm going to be

7

up on the Navajo Reservation, which is all strange country to me, Bob thought you might be able to give me a few pointers."

While Longarm spoke, Mae Blaisdell had been studying him. "You don't look to me like a man who needs any pointers," she said. "Seems to me you could take care of yourself just about anywhere."

Two short blasts from the locomotive whistle sounded before Longarm could reply.

Grey said, "We've got up steam, I guess. I'll leave you two to get on board, while I get the other passengers to start moving."

"If you'd like to sit with me while we ride back to Gallup, I'll try to tell you whatever I can about Navajo country, Marshal Long," Mae offered.

"That's right nice of you, ma'am," Longarm replied. "And I'll just take that invitation. Which car are you in?"

"That one." She pointed. "In the middle."

They walked over to the vestibule and Longarm gave her a hand up the steps. They settled down on a green plush seat, disturbing the fuzzy fibers enough to raise the faint aroma of coal soot that was always present on the seats of railroad cars. They'd barely gotten seated when the train began backing out of the cut and for the first few minutes they said nothing, looking out the window at the rugged faces of the broken boulders sliding past the window. Then they were out of the cut and rumbling along the trestle again.

Mae Blaisdell turned from the window, and Longarm said, "I was surprised when Bob Grey told me you were an Indian trader, Mrs. Blaisdell. It seems to me like that's a kind of unusual thing for a woman to be doing. Do you run the trading post all by yourself?"

"Well, not exactly. You see, Navajos don't like to trade with a woman. My clerk, Hosteen Clau, handles the trading. I might step in if there's a woman trading for flour or lard or something like that, but I try to be as inconspicuous as I can when there's any serious trading being done with a Navajo man."

"If you don't mind my asking, Mrs. Blaisdell, how'd you happen to get into being an Indian trader?"

8

"'Happen' is about the right word, Marshal Long. My husband got the idea that a trading post up in the northern part of the reservation would be a profitable thing. So he quit his job with the Indian Bureau about five years ago and we moved up there. Then, just over two years after we'd settled there, Fred was killed when his horse fell over the rim of an arroyo. Everything we had in the world was in that trading post, so I didn't have much choice but to keep it going."

"I hope you're doing well."

"Oh, I'm not complaining. I don't expect Shonto will ever make me rich, the way Lorenzo Hubbell's getting on his big post at Ganado on the east side of the reservation, but Hubbell had a five-year start on Fred and me."

"Bob Grey might've mentioned the name of the town where your business is, but if he did, I disremember it."

She smiled. "The trading post's called Shonto, Marshal, and it's a long way from being a town. There's no real town on the reservation north of Ganado. The Navajos don't build towns. They like to keep their *hogans* away from anything that resembles a settlement."

"Sounds to me like a right lonesome place."

"It is. I suppose I ought to be glad for this delay in getting back. It's a chance to stay in a town a while longer and see something besides Indians and bare country."

"Well, I got a lot of questions I'd like to ask you about the lay of the land up where you are now, but there won't be time for me to get around to all of 'em before we get off the train. Maybe we can have supper together."

Mae looked at Longarm for a moment, then smiled. "You know, Marshal, you're the first man who's asked me to dinner in two years. And I think I'd enjoy it very much indeed."

Chapter 2

Longarm and Mae Blaisdell sat over their coffee in the dining room of the Harvey House. They'd both lost the stiffness that had been apparent during the early part of their dinner after she had interrupted one of Longarm's questions with a smile and a raised hand and said, "You don't strike me as being a formal kind of man, Marshal. My name's Mae, and it's a lot easier to say than Mrs. Blaisdell. I suppose you have a first name, too?"

"Why, sure, Mae. It's Custis, only none of my friends ever call me by it. Mostly, they call me Longarm."

After a momentary frown, she'd nodded. "Of course—the long arm of the law. Well, go on, Longarm. What were you about to ask me?"

"When we was talking on the train about your trading post, you said Shonto wasn't really a town."

"It's not. I can see three or four Navajo houses—they call them *hogans*—when I look out my front door, and in the draws within a couple of miles around my place there are perhaps another eight or ten *hogans* tucked away, but that's all."

"Then how come you and your husband set up your post there?"

"It's as good a place as any. I suppose we could've gone to the Hopi Reservation, which is right in the middle of the Navajo lands. But the Navajos and Hopis aren't friendly toward each other. In fact, there's a treaty between them that they won't trespass on each other's reservations."

"Does that mean you don't get any Hopi business?"

"Well, like all treaties, this one has some loopholes. They don't count a visit to a trading post as trespassing."

"What about the Hopis?" Longarm asked. "Don't they live in towns either?"

"They live in pueblos, most of them quite a way from Shonto, in the middle of the Hopi reservation. There's a whole cluster of them there: Oraibi, Walpi, Polacca, Jeddito. And there's one near Shonto; it's called Tonalea. But about all the Hopis have to trade is garden produce and pottery."

"Are they like all the Indians I've run into? Outside of the tribes back east in the Nation, I never did see Indians that had much money to spend."

Mae shrugged. "The Hopis and Navajos certainly don't have much money. I can just about count on my fingers the cash sales I make in a year's time."

"I guess you have to carry a pretty good stock of stuff."

"Except that I trade instead of selling for cash, my place isn't much different from a general store. I carry the same kind of merchandise, everything from dry goods to hardware."

"What do you trade for, mostly, Mae?"

"Wool and horses. The Navajo women weave beautiful blankets, and they always have a lot of raw wool they can't use. Some of the men have started silversmithing. They melt down dollars and make bracelets and belt buckles. Their horses aren't much, but I can sell them in Flagstaff or in the ranching country around Prescott."

"What about the blankets and the silver stuff?"

"Oh, I can turn them to a good profit in Albuquerque and Santa Fe. Fred always had it in mind to try shipping to El Paso and San Antonio, but he died before he could start doing that and I've never been able to find the time to try."

"Seems to me those places are pretty far off from Shonto."

"They are," Mae said. "In a way, I'm glad we had to stop here in Gallup. It'll give me a chance to take a closer look at the town tomorrow morning. I've been thinking about opening an Indian goods store here."

"Why not in Winslow? It'd be closer."

"Of course, but this is a bigger town, and there are already a couple of stores in Winslow that carry Indian trade goods." Mae glanced around the big beamed room, empty now except for themselves and a few waiters clearing the deserted tables. The pinon-wood fire that had danced in the huge lava rock fireplace which dominated one end of the room had died away to a glow of coals. She said, "I think we're overstaying our welcome."

Longarm looked around the dining room and nodded. "I imagine the help'd like to see us leave about now. I'll tell you what, Mae. Let's take a little stroll around town. Maybe you'll see something that'd save you time in looking around tomorrow."

"I'd like that. Usually I'm in such a hurry to get back after I've taken a load of trade goods to Albuquerque that I just don't have time to stop here."

They went outside and walked slowly through the grounds of the Harvey House to the street. Like most small settlements of the frontier West, Gallup was a one-street town, though its main street wasn't typical of most. Instead of being lined on both sides with business buildings, the Santa Fe depot, offices, roundhouse, shop, and sidings all stood on the north side of the street. They extended on the west far beyond the limited number of business buildings on the south side, which had the effect of stretching the single street to an abnormal length.

Nor were the business buildings that faced the Santa Fe complex typical of the West. Instead of being frame construction, most of them were built of dark red brick or rosy-pink sandstone. The difference even extended to the sidewalks, which were made of flagstones instead of boards.

However, the stores were those Longarm had seen in every other small Western town he'd ever visited. There were two general stores, a bank, a pharmacy, a restaurant in which they could see a Chinese cook at work, a doctor's office, and a dry-goods shop. There were also half a dozen saloons strung out along the unpaved thoroughfare, and the usual complement of drunks clustered in front of them.

Longarm and Mae strolled slowly, taking their time, talking but little after their prolonged conversation during dinner. Mae slowed their progress by asking Longarm to stop and wait while she peered into the dark interiors of several of the stores, trying to see what kind of Indian goods they stocked.

Gallup had not reached the stage of installing street lights as yet. The only light on the street was that which spilled through the windows or open doors of the stores still open, and the night lights in the few stores that took such a precaution. Still, Mae managed to see inside some of the establishments, and Longarm waited patiently, puffing on the cheroot he'd lighted as they left the hotel grounds, while she pressed her face to the windows or the glass door panels and looked.

They reached the livery stable at the western end of the street and started back, walking faster now, since Mae's curiosity had already been satisfied. After they'd passed the cut red stone building occupied by the Bank of Gallup, Longarm stopped in the middle of the intersecting street.

"What's wrong?" she asked.

"I ain't sure." Longarm frowned. "It seems like to me that there was a night light showing inside that bank when we passed this way the first time."

"Was there? I remember looking in and seeing the dial on the safe, but I don't remember a light."

"Stands to reason there was one if you saw the safe."

"Yes, I suppose there must've been. And I *did* see the safe because I remember thinking how big its dial was compared to the one on my little safe at Shonto. Why, Longarm?"

"Because there's not any light in there now."

"Do you think somebody might have been in there, working late, when we passed before?"

"If there had been, you'd have seen 'em."

"Then—"

Longarm interrupted. "Then somebody's in there now, and they don't want anybody passing by to see 'em. Which means whoever's inside is likely robbing the bank."

He took Mae's arm and led her quickly to the corner

opposite the one where the bank stood. He stopped when they passed the end of the brick wall of the store that occupied the corner.

"Now, you stay right here," he told her. "Don't get out from behind this wall."

"But, Longarm, shouldn't you go find a constable or a deputy sheriff or somebody? There might be a gang inside the bank, if it's really being robbed."

"I misdoubt I'd find any local lawman in time to be of much help," he replied. "And I'll bet there ain't more'n two or three men inside. It takes a gang to hold up a bank, but it don't take but one man to open a safe, and a good one can work a combination in the dark. Now you stay here and keep behind this wall, where you'll be safe."

Before Mae could protest, Longarm was crossing the street to the bank. He stopped in the cover of its front wall and stooped low when he passed in front of the window on his way to the door. Very quietly, he reached for the doorknob and tried it. The knob turned easily, but the door did not open when he pushed against it.

Avoiding the window again, Longarm went to the side of the building, where he'd seen a second door when he crossed the street. Cautiously, he turned the knob. Like the one on the front door, it turned readily. But unlike the front door, the side door swung inward when he pushed carefully against it.

There's somebody in there, all right, old son, Longarm told himself silently. *And there ain't but one thing they'd be doing at night this way, without a light inside. But once their eyes get used to the dark, there'd be enough spill in from the street to let 'em find their way around.*

Thinking of night vision gave Longarm an idea. Before drawing his Colt, he took half a dozen wooden matches from his pocket and bundled them tightly between his left thumb and forefingers. Sliding his Colt from its worn-slick holster, he pressed against the door with the hands holding the matches.

A scraping of leather bootsoles on a tiled floor gave Longarm notice that his guesses had been good. Squeezing his eyes tightly closed, he pushed the door wide open,

14

scraping the heads of the matches along the doorframe with the same movement. The matches flared brightly, their combined flame shining yellow through Longarm's closed eyelids. Keeping his eyes shut, he dropped flat as the matches flared, and held the burning bundle well away from his body as he went down.

A shotgun roared out and its pellets peppered the doorway above Longarm. Thanks to his precautions, Longarm's head and body were out of the pattern of the gun's pellets, but he felt a searing sting on his outstretched arm just before he landed on the floor, his eyes open and his Colt ready.

With his eyes blinded by the flaring match-heads, the person with the shotgun triggered the second barrel without changing its point of aim. The pellets spattered into the doorframe and the wall beside it, but most of them went harmlessly out the open door.

Longarm had been expecting the second blast, and had opened his eyes only as slits. He saw the silhouettes of two men outlined against the wide black door of the safe, and could pick the one holding the shotgun as his first target. His forefinger tightened on the trigger of his Colt as he swung its muzzle. When he judged the muzzle to be in line with his target, Longarm fired.

Without waiting to see the effect of his slug, Longarm pushed himself forward in a froglike leap while he loosed his second slug, a blind shot at the spot where he'd glimpsed the second bank robber. He heard the grisly thunk of lead striking flesh, followed by a yell of pain.

"Damn it, Skag, I stopped one!" a man's voice exclaimed from the direction of the safe. "Get that shotgun!"

Longarm's third shot ricocheted off the safe's steel door with a muffled scratching. He changed position again. He was far enough inside the door now to be able to roll to one side. He finished his roll and fired a fourth time, aiming in the direction from which he'd heard the exclamation.

For a moment following the Colt's quick roar the silence inside the bank was unbroken. Then the man who'd spoken before whispered hoarsely, "Skag!" After a moment passed without a reply, he repeated, this time questioningly, "Skag?"

Straining, Longarm tried to peer through the darkness to locate the speaker, but all that he could see in the almost total darkness of the bank's interior was the darker blob of the safe door across the room. There were pieces of furniture—desks, he guessed—that kept him from seeing anything at floor level.

"Skag?" the unknown voice called again, querulously.

Longarm decided he'd risk little by speaking. His arm was smarting now where the buckshot pellets had hit him, and he could feel wetness spreading along the sleeve of his flannel shirt. He debated for a moment, then decided that since he hadn't heard the click-slip-snap of a shotgun being broken to reload, the speaker was either without a gun or too badly wounded to shoot.

Before saying anything, Longarm cut his risk by changing position again, and rolled a few feet away. While he scooped cartridges from his coat pocket and reloaded, he said, "Your friend Skag's most likely dead. Either that or he's hurt too bad to talk."

"That's a lie!" the unseen man rasped. When Longarm didn't answer, and the other repeated, his tone now one of fearful concern, "Skag? Skag, why in hell don't you say something?"

Longarm finished reloading and said sternly, "I'm a U. S. Marshal, and I've just showed you that I can hit a target in the dark. Now, are you ready to surrender to me, or do you want me to shoot you, too?"

"A U. S. Marshal?" the voice asked from the darkness. "How in hell do I know that?"

"I've got a badge to prove it, but I can't show it to you in the dark, so I guess you'll just have to take my word for it."

"You swear you won't shoot me if I give up?"

"You got my word."

"All right. I'm throwing in my hand."

"Strike a match so I can see you," Longarm ordered.

"Damn it, if I had a match, don't you think I'd've struck it before now? Anyhow, Skag's the one that does the shooting."

Longarm thought for a moment while he looked around,

16

still trying without any success to see the speaker. He decided to take the final step. He braced himself to jump to his feet with no lost time or motion. Then, fishing out another match, he struck it, and as its head burst into flame, flicked the flaring match high in the air.

As he tossed the match up, Longarm moved. The glimpse he got of the room before the flame fizzled out showed him that the other man was sitting on the floor, his back to the wall at one side of the safe, his legs stretched in front of him. The still, sprawled body of the robber Longarm had shot lay on the floor a pace or two beyond the spot where the live one was sitting.

In three quick steps, Longarm was at the bank robber's side, the cold muzzle of his Colt pressed to the man's temple. "All right! Hand over your gun!" he snapped.

"Damn it, I can't draw it. It's in my holster. I'll lean over so you can get at it, if you'll hold me up."

Longarm managed to get another match out of his pocket and scratched it on the wall. The dark eyes of the man on the floor gazed up at him from a face that was cadaverously white and thin. He was holding his right hand over the biceps of his left arm. Longarm lowered the match and saw that the man's right hand had been sheared to a narrow triangle. Only the little finger remained.

"We never butted heads before, but I know who you are," he told his prisoner. "One-finger Smith. Hell, Smith, I thought you'd still be in prison."

"I just been out a month," Smith confessed. "And I wish you'd hold off from talking until you get my arm tied up. If I let go of it, I'm likely to bleed to death."

Longarm felt the match he held beginning to burn his fingers and let it fall to the floor. He struck another and looked for a lamp.

"The night light's just the other side of the safe," Smith said. "Go ahead, Marshal. You can see I ain't in no condition to hurt you."

"Just the same, I'll take your gun."

Bending over Smith, Longarm pulled the wounded robber's revolver out of its holster, then stepped over and with the last flicker of the match flame lighted the night lamp.

17

It gave off only a feeble glow, but to Longarm, his eyes widely dilated from being in the darkness, the glimmer seemed as bright as sunlight at high noon. He looked at Smith. The robber was gazing at the sprawled body on the floor.

"I'd damn near as soon be the one you shot," he told Longarm bitterly. "Skag didn't want to do this job. He wanted for us to go on West and—"

Longarm never did find out what the dead robber had wanted, for before Smith could finish, Mae Blaisdell burst into the room followed by a husky man who had a star pinned to his vest and a shotgun in his hands. They stopped just inside the door after seeing Longarm with his Colt still in his hand, the body on the floor, and the wounded Smith immobilized against the wall.

"Are you all right, Longarm?" Mae gasped breathlessly. She saw the wet stains glistening on his coat sleeve and asked, "You got shot, didn't you?"

"Nothing I can't stand, Mae," Longarm said.

"Maybe you better tell me what happened," the man who'd come in with Mae suggested. "I'm Joe Kleber, the town marshal. The lady's already told me who you are."

"There ain't all that much to tell," Longarm said. "And if it's all the same to you, Kleber, I'll stop in at your jail and tell you about it in the morning. I got a buckshot or two in my arm, and they're getting a mite uncomfortable."

"Why, sure, Marshal Long. Whatever you say. I guess this one that's still sitting up will go to jail, and I'll get the undertaker to take care of the dead one."

"That'll be fine," Longarm nodded. "The one sitting up is One-finger Smith—only I don't expect Smith was the name he begun with when he was born. But he'll need to have a doctor look at him. He claims he's bleeding pretty bad."

"What about you?" Mae broke in. "You're bleeding, too! You need a doctor yourself! What in the world—"

"All I got is a scratch or two," Longarm told her. "And I can fix myself up better than any doctor can. Come on, Mae. We've had enough excitement for tonight. Let's go

18

back to the Harvey House, and after I've had a swallow of Maryland rye and put a bandage on, I'll tell you all about it."

Chapter 3

"You can't put a bandage on your own arm!" Mae protested. "That's a job that takes two hands."

"I'll manage," Longarm replied.

"No, I'll manage," she said quickly. "I've bandaged gunshot wounds before, and a little bit of blood doesn't bother me."

"Now, look here—" he began.

As though he hadn't spoken, Mae went on. "I hope you've got a clean shirt in your room. If the condition of your coat sleeve means anything, you're going to need a shirt to wear while I'm mending the one you've got on."

"I generally carry a spare shirt when I'm travelling on a case," Longarm replied.

They'd reached the grounds of the Harvey House by now, and started along the cinder walkway leading to the hotel's entrance. The big chandeliers that hung from the ceiling had been turned off, and only a subdued light spilled from the wide double doors. Most of the windows of the rooms on the two upper floors were dark. They started up the path to the lobby steps.

"Now, look here, Mae," Longarm protested as they went into the hotel. "All I aimed to do was to walk back here with you and make sure you got to your room safe. You don't have to put yourself out taking care of me."

"Your arm needs attention, Longarm."

"Not all that much. It hurts a little bit, but I can stand it till I got time to take care of it. A man that holds down

20

a job like mine gets used to looking out for himself."

"But doesn't your wife—"

"Mae, I ain't got a wife."

"You're not married, then?"

"Of course not. Never have been, and ain't aiming to be."

"Then, that's all the more reason for me to help you. Now, I'll see if the hotel doesn't have an old pillowcase or something I can make a bandage of, and you—"

"I already know what I'm going to do. Seeing as the Harvey House is temperance, I'm going back to that saloon we passed up the street a minute ago and get myself a bottle of Tom Moore. Right now, what I need most is a drink of good Maryland rye, and a cigar, which I got plenty of in my pocket." When Mae did not reply, but just tilted her chin up and stared straight ahead, Longarm went on, "I wasn't aiming to hurt your feelings, Mae. It ain't that I don't appreciate what you want to do, but—"

"If that's not just like a man!" she interrupted. "You say one thing and mean something else!"

"I didn't mean anything else!" But Longarm had seen the look in Mae's eyes in the eyes of other women, and had learned to give in gracefully. "All right," he said. "If it'll make you feel better, I'll be real grateful to you for fixing up my arm." Then he added hastily, "And my shirt."

"Good. Now go back to that saloon and have your drink. Be sure to get the bottle of whiskey, too. I'll need something to use for a disinfectant. I'll get the cloth I need, one way or another. I'm in Room 214. I'll leave the door on the latch so you won't have to knock."

Longarm stayed in the saloon just long enough to swallow one drink and buy the bottle of Tom Moore he'd promised himself. Longarm tucked the bottle under his arm and started back to the hotel. He'd been gone less than a quarter of an hour. Ignoring the curious glance of the desk clerk, he went up the stairs and opened the door to Mae's room.

She had taken off her jacket and sat in her billowing white linen shirtwaist beside a small table. On the table lay strips of white cloth torn from the pillowcase that lay on the floor beside it. Also lying on the table was a small pair

21

of scissors and a horn-handled pocketknife.

"I wasn't sure you'd really come back," Mae told Long-arm.

"I told you I would," he said, setting the bottle of Tom Moore on the table. "And I generally do what I say I will."

Mae stood up with a gesture at the table. "Now that you're back with the whiskey, we might as well get started. Take off your coat and shirt, and I'll see how bad your arm is."

"I keep telling you, it ain't bad at all," Longarm said. But he slid out of his coat and turned his back while he took the derringer attached to his watch chain and dropped it into the pocket that held the watch. He shed his vest and hung it over the back of the chair on which he'd laid his coat, unbuckled his gunbelt and hung it over the same chair, then began to unbutton his bloodstained shirt.

Mae looked at the arm of the shirt. There were three small rips in it, two in the forearm and one just above the elbow. Longarm got the shirt off and handed it to her. While he unbuttoned his balbriggans, Mae sat down and spread the arm of the shirt across her lap.

"It's not as bad as I was afraid it would be," she said.

"I told you I didn't get more'n a scratch."

Longarm pulled the wounded arm out of the sleeve of his balbriggans. As the sleeve drooped to the floor a pellet of buckshot rolled out. Longarm ignored the ugly little lead ball and looked at his left arm.

Three buckshot pellets had hit him. One had grazed his upper arm just above the elbow, leaving a shallow two-inch crease that was now covered with crusted blood. Another pellet had gone through the flesh of his forearm an inch or so below the elbow. This was the shot that now lay on the floor. The third ball had hit the bottom side of his forearm and ploughed under the skin and a thin layer of flesh. It was still in his arm, making a bulge at the spot where it had stopped.

"I told you I wasn't hurt very bad," Longarm said, turning and extending his arm for Mae to look at. He caught a quick glimpse of her face as he turned. She had not been looking

22

at his wounded arm, but at the expanse of his chest revealed by the half-removed undersuit. Her eyes were fixed on the coat of thick brown curls over his chest and the muscles that rippled under them as he moved.

Mae dropped her eyes quickly to inspect the wounds. She said, "The one shot that's still in there won't be hard to get out. And I can open the wound where one went through, and disinfect it. All the other one needs is to be washed clean."

"I'd better open that bottle, if you're ready to start."

Conscious of Mae's eyes on him, Longarm lifted the bottle by its neck, gave the bottom a hard thwack with the heel of his hand to force the cork out a fraction of an inch, then bit down on the protruding end of the cork and twisted the bottle to finish opening it. He took a swallow of the pungent rye before handing the bottle to Mae, and turned to the chair where his coat lay to get a cheroot from its pocket. His back still toward her, he lighted the cheroot.

When he turned, Mae had removed her blouse. Her bare shoulders gleamed with a silken white luster in the light of the lamp that stood on the bureau. Her camisole was made of some thin gauzy material, and the jutting tips of her full breasts made tiny peaks in the fabric. Through the thin veil of cloth he could see the dark circles of their rosettes.

"I hope you don't mind," Mae said, nodding toward the blouse which she'd tossed over the back of her chair. "My blouse is so full-cut that it would just get in my way."

"I don't mind at all," Longarm told her. He held out his arm. "You go on and do whatever you got a mind to."

Mae took his wrist in one hand and ran the warm palm of the other up his forearm and biceps. Her palm was slightly moist, and Longarm sensed rather than saw the tiny quiver that shook her shoulders as she stroked his skin. "I'll be as quick as I can," she said.

Moistening a piece torn from the pillow slip with the whiskey, Mae mopped the wounds and the skin around them. She picked up the knife, opened its small blade, and wiped the metal carefully with the whiskey-soaked cloth. Then she sat down.

"Hold on to the back of the chair," she told Longarm. "I'm going to take out that buckshot, and it'll probably hurt a bit."

Longarm gripped the chair back and clamped his teeth hard on his cheroot. Mae made a single quick cut above the bulge that marked the buckshot pellet. Longarm felt the sting of the knife, then Mae let the blade fall to the floor and squeezed gently on the flesh below the cut. The lead ball popped out and fell into her lap.

Her hands moving quickly, Mae mopped the cut with a newly wetted pad of cloth. The alcohol in the rye bit Longarm's flesh, but he held his arm rigidly still. Mae asked him, "Do you want to stop a minute before I take care of that hole the other buckshot made?"

"No. Go on and finish," he told her calmly.

Pouring alcohol on the tip of the knife, Mae lifted the flap of skin at one end of the second wound. She tilted the whiskey bottle to let a trickle of the liquor seep into the hole that was left when the pellet passed through. This time, Longarm felt the bite of whiskey for a full minute, but still he did not flinch. She put the knife down and with quick efficiency wrapped strips of cloth around the two wounds in his forearm. After knotting them firmly in place, she looked up at Longarm and smiled.

"Well?" she asked. "How does it feel?"

"It smarts a little bit, but not so bad I can't stand it." Longarm puffed at his cheroot and found that he'd bitten through the stub that remained. He tossed the dead cigar on the little heap of used cloth on the table and lighted a fresh one, then tilted the whiskey bottle and had a large, satisfying swallow.

Mae held out her hand. "I think I could stand a drink of that myself." Longarm handed her the bottle. She took a small swallow and exhaled gustily, then, with her mouth still puckered, went on, "I suppose I'll feel better when it begins to take effect."

"Sure you will," Longarm assured her. He reached for his shirt, but Mae caught his arm and stopped him.

"I told you I'd rinse the blood off your shirt and mend the holes," she said. "I'll rinse your underwear, too."

"Now, you don't expect me to take off—" Longarm began.

"No. Just stand over there by the washstand, close enough for me to get the sleeve in the washbowl."

She went over to the small oak stand and Longarm followed her. Mae poured water into the bowl and placed the pitcher on the floor. She took the sleeve of Longarm's balbriggans and tugged at the knitted fabric. Longarm was too tall for the sleeve to go into the washbowl. He bent over. Mae turned her back to him and gave the arm of the balbriggans another tug.

Her tugging at the sleeve forced Longarm to bend still further, and he put his right hand on the washstand to keep his balance. His biceps were brushing Mae's arms now, his chest pressed firmly into the warm, soft skin of her back and shoulders. She leaned forward to push the sleeve into the washbowl, and her movement pushed her soft buttocks and thighs back against Longarm's crotch. As Mae's arms moved, rubbing the balbriggans' sleeve in the bowl, her buttocks swayed from side to side.

Feeling the warmth of her skin on the insides of his biceps and the pressure of her moving buttocks against his groin, Longarm began to grow hard. He responded to her silent overtures by pressing his growing erection firmly against her gently swaying buttocks.

Mae looked over her shoulder. "What have you been waiting for, Longarm? I was beginning to wonder if you expected me to send you an engraved invitation."

"I just waited long enough to make sure," he told her. He brought up his hands and cupped them around her generous breasts, slightly pendulous now that she was leaning forward. As he began caressing them he added, "And you were so busy—"

"I'm not that busy now." Mae wrung out the sleeve and let it fall. Her hands worked for a quick moment at the buttons on the side placket of her skirt, then she pulled her camisole out of the skirt and pushed the skirt down to her thighs. "And I don't want to wait any longer. Feeling you get hard against my ass has got me so hot I can't stand it! Hurry up, Longarm! Go in, right now!"

Longarm had started unbuttoning his trousers when Mae first turned to look back at him. He let them drop now and pushed his balbriggans below his hips, freeing his erection. Mae spread her legs and caught her breath as she felt Longarm's tip rub along the crease of her buttocks. She bent forward again and spread her thighs. Longarm slid between them, his fingers meeting her warm, slick wetness as he guided himself into her. Mae's entire body quaked as Longarm began his penetration.

"Oh, God!" she gasped. "I didn't know how big you are! I've never felt anything like this, Longarm! Don't stop, just go in slower!"

Longarm did stop, but only for a few seconds. Then he did as she'd requested, sliding in slowly but steadily while Mae arched her back. Longarm's hands sought her breasts again, and Mae reached up to slip the straps of her camisole off her shoulders. She shrugged the flimsy undergarment down to free her breasts for Longarm's questing hands. He rubbed her hard, protruding nipples with his roughened fingers, and Mae groaned happily and heaved her hips higher in response to the new sensations that were racing along her nerves.

Longarm began stroking. He thrust slowly and shallowly at first, and Mae writhed her hips from side to side and up and down until he increased his speed as well as the depth of his penetration. Her breath was being torn from her throat in sharp, welling sobs.

"I can't wait for you, Longarm!" she wailed. "I'm just about to— Oh, God, I am, I am, right now!"

"Go on and take your pleasure, Mae," Longarm said. "It's going to take me a while yet."

He went into her full length and pulled her hips hard against him, then held her firmly while her moans dissolved into a series of high, sharp yelps. Her hips waggled faster and faster in spite of Longarm's hands holding them to his groin. With a final cry and a spasmodic jerk that almost pulled her free from Longarm's grasp, she reached her climax. He kept holding her against him while the spasmodic gyrations of her body grew fainter and fainter and at last stopped entirely.

26

After a few moments Mae sighed and, as the pent-up breath escaped said, "Oh, that really shook me! I've just been without a man too long, that's what my trouble is. Don't let yourself get soft, now, Longarm. I love that feeling of having you in me so much that I don't want to lose it."

"You don't need to worry," Longarm assured her. "I got a lot of time left before I'll start shriveling up."

"Can you stay hard while we get these damn clothes off and move over to the bed?"

"Sure. You want to move now?"

"As soon as you're ready."

Longarm pulled away from Mae and she turned to face him, her camisole bunched just above her hips, her skirt draped over the tops of her low slip-on boots. Longarm was tempted to smile, but resisted the temptation until Mae began grinning at him. He was naked from his head to his boot-tops, his balbriggans and trousers swaddled in an untidy heap around his feet. He grinned back at her.

"Do you need help getting untangled?" she asked, struggling to free her legs.

Longarm stopped his efforts to lever out of his boots while still standing up and told her, "If you'll just put that chair behind me, I'll be all right."

Both naked at last, they moved with arms entwined across the room to the bed. Mae flung back the folded counterpane and blankets, saying, "They'll just be in the way." She let herself fall to the bed, then spread her arms. "Hurry, Long-arm. Every time I look at you I start twitching inside."

"If you feel that way, it's time to start curing it."

Longarm did not hurry, this time. He positioned himself between Mae's wide-open thighs and let her guide him into her. But after a few minutes of hard stroking he changed his pace and, instead of continuing to thrust with full-length strokes, as her breathless cries urged him to do, he went in shallowly. He held himself away from her, lifting his body just enough to frustrate her efforts to jounce her hips higher and take him deeper.

"You're teasing me, Longarm!" she whispered accusingly, after her third effort to engulf him had failed. "And I'm burning up inside! Give me what I need!"

27

Longarm had been letting himself build with his me-
thodical, shallow penetrations, and he was ready to respond.
He speeded up the tempo of his thrusts and went deeper and
deeper each time he sunk into Mae. Her hips rose to meet
him and her buttocks gyrated wildly as she matched his
quicker stroking. By the time Longarm was almost at the
point of no return, Mae was already beyond control.

Mae gave herself up to sensation as Longarm continued
to drive hard and fast. She heaved beneath him, each breath
bringing a happy whimper from her throat.

Longarm reached his orgasm a moment later. He thrust
hard against her quivering body as he jetted again and again,
until the languor of fulfillment took him.

"You're not going to leave me, are you?" Mae whispered
to him after their bodies had grown calm.

"Not unless you want me to."

"And you won't mind if I wake you up later?"

"Not a bit," he told her through the beginning of a yawn.

"Good. Then—" Mae's voice trailed off into silence.

Longarm waited for a moment for her to finish. When
he realized what had stopped her words, he let sleep claim
him, too.

Chapter 4

"Will you be coming up to Shonto pretty soon, Longarm?" Mae asked as they stood on the platform of the Santa Fe's pint-sized depot at Winslow. The train from which they had just alighted was already pulling away.

"It's hard to tell. I don't know a thing about this case I was sent here on, Mae. I think I told you that."

"Yes. And I haven't asked you any questions because I know men don't like women to poke into their business. But I do hope I'll see you again."

"I don't need to tell you I feel the same way. If my job takes me up where your trading post is, I'll sure stop in. But I guess you know the job comes first."

"Of course. Well, you keep in mind what I told you about how to find the place."

"Oh, I ain't going to forget. Don't worry about that."

Mae stood indecisively for a moment. She looked past Longarm to the edge of the depot platform, where the young Navajo who'd taken her bags when she got off the train sat waiting in a long-bed wagon. Then she said, "I guess I'd better not keep Hosteen Clau waiting any longer. He's already waited long enough, thanks to that rock slide. But I— well, it sure wouldn't make me mad if I lost another day, provided it ended like yesterday did."

"Neither would I," Longarm replied. "But you've got work to do, and so have I. It's time now for both of us to go on with our business and wait till next time."

Mae nodded. She started to turn away, hesitated, and

29

said, "I'm not going to say goodbye, Longarm. I've just got a hunch that somehow or other you will be up in Shonto before you leave."

"There's a pretty good chance of it, I guess. So, I'll see you then, Mae."

Mae nodded and walked slowly to the wagon. Longarm waited until the Navajo had started away from the depot before he went over to the ticket window and asked where the Indian Bureau office was located. In a town the size of Winslow, finding the building was no problem. All Longarm needed to do was to walk down the street the clerk had named until he saw the familiar dark brown paint which was the uniform color applied to frame Federal buildings everywhere.

Tom Armbruster, the agent in charge of the Navajo and Hopi Reservations, was a younger man than Longarm had expected to see in such a big job. Armbruster was also quite a bit more forthright and decisive than most of the Indian Bureau employees with whom Longarm had come into contact.

"I'll hand you the straight facts, Marshal Long," Armbruster said after the introductions were over. "I don't know what kind of mess you're going to run into when you start your investigation up there on the tribal lands."

"Maybe if you tell me why you sent for me, I'd know a little bit more about what to expect," Longarm suggested. "What laws have the Indians been breaking that'd make the Indian Bureau ask the Federal marshal's force for help?"

"That's the problem," the Indian agent replied. "I can't even say for sure that a law's been broken or any kind of crime committed."

Longarm looked up from the cheroot he was lighting to see if Armbruster was joking, but the agent's face was sober. Through the smoke from his cheroot, Longarm asked, "If you ain't even sure of that much, then why'd you call for help?"

"The acting chief in our Denver regional office wanted an investigation by an agency that has no connection with the Indian Bureau."

"You mean the buck's being passed, and I'm going to

30

find myself in trouble with two bosses instead of one, re-gardless of what I turn up?"

Armbruster smiled. "I like the way you put that, Marshal, but this honestly isn't a case of buck-passing."

"I'm listening. Go on and tell me why."

"Look at the map on the wall behind you," Armbruster said.

Longarm turned around in his chair and studied the big map. It took in roughly a quarter of Arizona Territory, a slice of New Mexico Territory to the east, and extended in a large arc into Utah Territory to the north. Blocked out in the center of this vast expanse was a rectangle that just missed being a square; it took up roughly one-fifth, Longarm estimated at a glance, of the whole area covered by the map.

"That's a pretty good-sized chunk of country," he said noncommittally as he turned back to face the agent.

"It looks a lot smaller on a map than it does when you're out in the middle of it trying to figure out which way to go," Armbruster said. "It takes up not quite a quarter, but substantially more than a fifth of the entire Territory. That little block in the middle of the map is Hopi land; the rest is Navajo."

"I figured." Longarm nodded. "But what's the size of the reservation got to do with why I'm here?"

"I don't know a hell of a lot about the U. S. Marshal's jurisdiction, but I assume it includes the entire country, when Federal law's been broken," Armbruster said. "How many men are there on your force, Marshal Long?"

"Why, I don't rightly know. There's nine of us and the chief marshal working out of the Denver office."

"Until a few weeks ago, I had exactly one agent I could assign to handle any kind of law-breaking on either reser-vation," Armbruster said. "I don't even have one now."

"Ain't there some sheriffs around here with deputies?"

"They're forbidden by law to make any arrests on a reservation unless it's of a fugitive they've chased onto Indian land. Oh, there are the Navajo Police, which means a total of eight men. But they're chiefly concerned with enforcing the Navajos' own tribal laws. Does that sound like the kind of job you'd dream of holding, Marshal?"

31

His voice dry, Longarm answered quickly, "No, sir, not for a minute! But the way you're beating around the bush, it sounds to me like that's the kind of job I'm walking into here."

Armbruster shook his head. "I'm sorry, Marshal. I'm not trying to spook you. I just want you to realize why we felt that we had to call you in."

"Suppose you get right down to cases," Longarm said. "If you don't mind my saying so, I ain't heard a single fact yet."

"Even when you've heard all the facts I know, you won't have heard much. But I can give you the main points in very few words. In the past two months, three men have died up in the Navajo country. Two of them were Navajos— both of them were elders of the tribe and held places on the Navajo council. The other one was Jack Foster, the Bureau deputy I mentioned a minute ago—the one who was responsible for law enforcement."

Longarm waited for the Indian agent to continue. When he did not, Longarm said, "You say they died. You mean they were murdered? Or was it accidental? Or what?"

"That's part of what you're going to have to find out, Marshal Long. It could've been anything. All three deaths were from rattlesnake bites, or what looked like rattlesnake bites. The Navajos claim their tribal elders were killed by the Hopis. I guess you know the two tribes are hereditary enemies. They've been enemies more years than we really know about."

"Well, I've run into a fair bunch of Indian tribes, and they all seem to have a fight going with some other tribe."

"Yes. And these tribal feuds are handed down from generation to generation; they never seem to die out."

Longarm nodded. "I've seen about the same thing: Comanches against the Pawnees, Crows against Cheyennes— I could keep on going for half a day."

"I suppose the Navajos and Hopis have been fighting ever since the Navajos moved to this part of the country, and I'm told that was more than four hundred years ago," Armbruster said. "If you can believe the old tales, the Navajos were worse than the Apaches, and even that far back the Hopis had settled down to be farmers. But I don't think I need to go on, Marshal Long. You seem to be well informed on the Indian tribes."

"I don't know all that much about the tribes hereabouts. If I recall, it was Kit Carson that tamed the Navajos, back in '64. That ain't such a long time ago, to Indians. Seems like I heard the Navajos had promised Kit Carson that they'd quit fighting forever, but I guess that's too much to expect of 'em, since they were fighters for such a long time."

"Since I've been in charge here, there hasn't been any open fighting between the Navajos and the Hopis." Armbruster frowned. "Oh, a few young Navajo hotheads with big ideas will harass a Hopi farm, but the Navajo Police take care of them. And there'll be rumors, but you can't pin them down. A man from one tribe or the other drops out of sight, and the whisper gets started that somebody from the other tribe killed him."

"Which I gather is about what you got on your hands now?"

"Very close to it, I'd say. The Navajos are positive the Hopis are responsible for killing Peter Logadi and Belai Begay—the two elders I mentioned—mainly because the Hopis call rattlesnakes their brothers, and make sort of minor gods out of them. I'm sure you've heard about their snake dance?"

"A little bit. But if the three men died from snakebite, how did the Navajos get around to calling it murder? Just because the Hopis know how to handle rattlers?"

"That's the big reason. But I'm not sure they really *were* bitten by rattlers, and neither are the Navajos."

"Can you explain why?"

"Because, according to Jack Foster's report, it'd have to have been one hell of a big rattlesnake to have its fangs spaced as far apart as the punctures were on the dead men. I thought you'd have seen that report. I sent a copy to the area chief in Denver."

"Nobody said a word to me about it. But if you got a copy handy, I guess I can look at it now."

"Oh, there's no need for you to waste your time on that. I can tell you whatever you might want to know."

"Why did Foster think the dead men weren't snakebit?"

"Something in the nature of the fang marks, Marshal. He wasn't really clear on that point. I intended to get him to add a little bit to clarify what he'd found, but Foster died before I got around to it."

"Is that all you have to go on?"

"Not quite. From what I've been told, all three men were bitten—if that's what you want to call it—in almost the same spot: just above the middle of the thigh, on the inside."

"Rattlers generally don't strike a man much higher than his knee when he's standing up," Longarm said thoughtfully. "Most of the time even lower'n that. Ankle-high is about right."

"Yes. That occurred to me."

"Sounds to me like you ain't quite sure yourself that those three men were snakebit," Longarm observed.

"I am—and I'm not. For one thing, if they were, it's one devil of a big coincidence to swallow."

"That's a bull's-eye," Longarm agreed. "But the first thing I'd want to know is whether all three had got crossways of them Hopis that knows how to handle rattlers."

"I can't tell you that," Armbruster said. "As far as I can find out, Jack didn't have any problems with them. But when I try to talk to the Navajos about the Hopis, I hit a stone wall."

"Which I ain't going to guarantee I can bust through."

"I don't really expect you to, Marshal Long. I suppose I'm really hoping what my chief in Denver hopes: that you've had enough experience with murder to sniff it out when you see it."

"Well, I've seen my share, I guess. But I've been surprised, and wrong almost as many times as I've been right."

"That's not what your superior thinks. Marshal Vail recommended you very highly."

"Well, that was nice of him, but when it comes to sniffing out a murderer, I ain't certain my nose is all that good."

Armbruster shrugged. "You'd do better than anyone else, I'm sure."

"Let's get back to the snakebites." Longarm frowned. "If they didn't come from a real, live rattler, how'd the fang marks get on the dead men's legs? And how in hell did they get where you said they were, up on the inside of their thighs?"

"Some of the Navajos say the marks came from an arrow with a pronged head that had been dipped in rattler venom."

"Hell's bells, Armbruster! Indians ain't used bows and arrows for fifty years or more!"

"I know." Armbruster nodded. "But I suppose it could've been done that way."

"Could have ain't the same as likely," Longarm said. He sat in silence for a moment. Then he said, "One thing I haven't found out yet. That reservation of yours is mighty damned big. Where'd these fellows die—or get killed? All three at about the same place, or quite a ways apart?"

"Nobody's sure where they were killed; that is, where the—well, call them fang wounds—were inflicted." Armbruster stood up and stopped over to the wall map. He placed a finger at the intersecting boundary lines that marked the northwestern corner of the Hopi Reservation. "This is White Mesa. It's one of the Hopi tribe's most sacred places. Black Mesa, on the northeastern corner of the reservation, is another one. Now, right here is the west arm of Moenkopi Wash, and this little stream about ten miles north of it is Kaibito Creek. Both the Navajos were found somewhere between the wash and the creek. Jack Foster's body was in the same general area. Just inside the Hopi Reservation boundary, between the east and west arms of Moenkopi Wash."

"I guess in this country you'd call that the same general area, all right," Longarm said. He'd spotted a familiar name on the map while following Armbruster's explanation. "That place called Shonto—I understand it's a trading post. On the train I met the lady who runs it."

"Mae Blaisdell," Armbruster nodded. "Her husband used to work for the Bureau. But I guess she'd have mentioned that."

"She did, as a matter of fact. He's been dead a while, she said."

"Yes. Heart trouble, I think. I know it was sudden. Why?"

"No reason. Her name just popped into my mind when I saw Shonto on the map."

"Well, you'll be close enough to drop in on her, if you feel like it. Oh, yes, there's someone else you might want to look in on, if you're in the vicinity. An English college professor—let's see, the name is . . ." Armbruster frowned, then said, "Cranborn. Professor R. M. Cranborn."

"Out after Indian relics, I guess?"

"Something like that. Has a camp on Black Mesa."

"Well, if I'm close by, I'll drop in."

Armbruster nodded. "Now, is there anything else you want to ask me about the killings? Not that I'm sure my answers would help much."

"If you've told me everything you know, I guess that's all I can expect, Armbruster. But there's a few things I need."

"A horse, I'm sure, and a map. A desert canteen, if you don't have one. And a Bureau voucher for your provisions. Anything else?"

"Not that I can think of, offhand. My saddle and other truck is over at the depot. I figure to buy my grub tonight and start out early tomorrow."

"If you think of something else, I live in the house right behind the office. Drop in if you want to talk some more before you ride out."

"Thanks. I guess there's a Harvey House in town?"

"There is, but you'll do as well for less money if you stay at Mrs. Farnsworth's place, the Arizona House. It's more a boardinghouse than a hotel, but it's clean and the food's good. Tell her you're here on Bureau business and she'll give you a special rate. Now I'll get my clerk to fix up those vouchers and dig out a map while I go out to the corral with you and pick out a horse."

Finding no real attractions in Winslow, Longarm decided to turn in early. The two saloons he'd visited after supper offered no Tom Moore or any other Maryland rye, and the substitute both barkeepers had offered, claiming it was sour-mash bourbon, had left him with a taste in his mouth as sour as the mash from which the liquor had been distilled.

He lighted a cheroot while he went up the stairs of the Arizona House and trailed a wreath of fragrant smoke behind him as he went down the hall. Unlocking the door of his room, he turned up the wick of the lamp he'd left burning on the bureau and washed out the taste of the bourbon with a swallow of Tom Moore from the bottle he'd bought in Gallup. Then, while finishing his cheroot, he made ready for the night.

Hanging his coat over the back of the chair beside the bureau, Longarm moved to the other chair at the head of the bed and hung his vest over it, his derringer in the lower fob pocket where it would be hidden but still handy. He draped his pistol belt over the head of the bed, where the butt of his .44 Colt was within easy reach. Only then did he finish undressing.

There was still a puff or two left in the cigar, and Longarm stepped over to the dresser for his nightcap. He was standing with the bottle of Maryland rye in one hand and the stub of the cheroot in the other, gazing at the sweep of his mustache, like the spread horns of a longhorn steer, when in the fly-specked mirror he thought he saw the bedclothes move.

Now, you ain't had all that much to drink, old son, he told himself, frowning, the nape of his neck prickling in response to the finely honed instincts that had saved him more than a few times in the past. *And there sure ain't no wind coming in through that closed window. Maybe under the bed—*

Stepping casually to the chair beside the bed, Longarm took the wicked little snub-nosed derringer from the pocket of the vest. He was about to drop flat and look under the bed when the bedspread moved again. And this time there was no mistaking it.

Longarm grabbed the corner of the spread and threw the covers toward the foot. There in the middle of the white sheet was the brown-and-tan coil of a big desert rattler. The snake was coiling, ready to strike.

Chapter 5

Longarm brought up the derringer and triggered it without aiming. The cone-nosed chunk of soft lead caught the side of the snake's body a handspan below its head. Thin blood mixed with shreds of flesh and snake scales spattered the white sheet. But, hurt as it was, the rattler was not yet dead. Even before the blast of sound from the derringer's muzzle had died away in the small room, the snake began coiling again, its jaws agape, its fangs two glistening, threatening arcs.

Longarm remembered that, even when mortally wounded, snakes take a long time to die. He fired the derringer's second barrel, aiming this time, and the rattler's head dissolved in a spray of white tissue, thin shards of bone, and drops of milky yellow venom. Though it was now headless, the snake's body continued to writhe and thrash around on the bed for several moments longer before subsiding into an intermittent twitching.

Heavy footsteps were pounding up the hall. Longarm slid into his trousers and draped his coat over his shoulders before slipping a fresh pair of cartridges into the derringer's barrels. Then he opened the door.

Two men were running toward his room from opposite directions. They saw the open door and stopped. Looking at the derringer in Longarm's hand, one of them asked, "You the one that done that shooting?"

Longarm nodded. "Found a rattlesnake in my room. Nothing to worry about now. It's dead."

Mrs. Farnsworth came bustling down the hall, still knotting the sash of the magenta wrapper she wore over a trailing nightgown. "Did I hear you say rattlesnake, Marshal Long?"

"You sure did, ma'am. I just shot one in my room."

"Well, praise the Lord, you killed it before it bit you."

"I'm afraid it sorta messed up the bed, though. The snake was in the middle of it, under the spread."

"Laws, don't bother about the bed! I'm just happy to see another one of those pesky rattlers dead!"

"You've had snakes come into the house before, then?" Longarm asked.

"Once—about a year ago. And nobody was bit that time, either. But, goodness knows, rattlers are as thick as flies at this time of the year." The landlady paused, then went on, "Now, I'll just move you to another room, Marshal, and leave this one for the housemaid to clean up tomorrow. There's a real nice room right down the hall here, and all you have to do is carry your things a few steps to get to it."

Settled into his new room after the excitement had subsided, Longarm stretched out on the bed, a freshly lighted cheroot in his mouth, the bottle of Tom Moore on a chair nearby. After swallowing a good sip of the smoothly biting rye, he lay staring at the geometric pattern of the tin-panelled ceiling and took stock.

Now, it could just have been accidental, old son, he told himself. *From what the landlady said, it wouldn't be stretching things too much. But there's snakes or snake poison already mixed up in this case, even if Armbruster wasn't too certain which was which. And being bit by a rattler sure wouldn't be a way I'd like to go.*

Longarm recalled the glimpse he'd had of the rattler's mouth in the seconds during which it was rearing to strike— tautly stretched cords of corpse-white tissue, toothless except for the curved fangs glistening in its upper jaw. A shudder crawled over his flesh. He took another drink and put the bottle back on the chair.

If somebody did put that snake in there to catch me when I crawled in bed, they'd have to've known what they was doing. But Winslow's just a little bitty town. It's the kind of place where everybody knows when a stranger comes in and where he's from and why he's come and where he's going. An awful lot of people know what I was sent here for.

Longarm thought of the people he'd encountered since beginning his trip to Arizona Territory who knew his identity and were aware that he was there on a case. The list started with the people in the Indian Bureau's Denver office, the Santa Fe train crew, the clerks under Armbruster at the local Indian Bureau office, Armbruster himself—and, as an after-thought, Mae Blaisdell.

Except she didn't know what kind of case I come here to work on, he reminded himself. *Still and all, it wouldn't have been too much of a trick for her to find out. And then there's that Indian driving her wagon, Hosteen something-or-other, she likely told him who I was and what I'm doing here. Hell, there might be fifteen or twenty people that could know, and it just might be that some of them don't want anybody poking into things. Guess about all a man can do in a fix like this is to keep his eyes and ears open and his mouth shut.*

Not satisfied, but realizing there was nothing he could do at the moment to dig out the answers to all the questions facing him, Longarm dropped the stub of his cheroot into the spittoon beside the bed and went to sleep.

Turning his eyes from the east, where the yellow-white glare of the morning sun sent white daggers stabbing into his eyes, Longarm looked ahead, to the north. He'd chosen his stopping place half a dozen miles back, when the winding trail that showed on his map as a dotted line took him out of the wide boulder-studded canyon onto a broad plateau. At the end of the plateau the little mesa atop which he now sat jutted like an upthrust fist from the flat ground around it.

Beyond the mesa, Longarm saw now, the trail he was taking north across the southern edge of Navajo land into the Hopi Reservation skirted what the map identified as the Hopi Buttes. They broke the horizon, already blurred and shimmering with heat-haze in spite of the early hour, as a ragged series of ledges, one rising above and behind the other, their faces even at this distance showing as layered, varicolored streaks.

Ahead of him and extending west from the buttes, the land levelled out. As far as he could see through the gathering heat-haze there was only sandy tan soil, almost void of vegetation, broken by small, rounded humps of hills and the flatter tops of many other mesas, some large, some small.

Longarm gazed farther to the west. He blinked and shook his head. Stretching to the western horizon, bathed in brilliant sunlight, he saw the broken country of the Painted Desert. He blinked again, taking in the riot of colors that ranged from purple-red through pink to brown and a dozen shades of lighter hues running the scale from dark tan to almost-pure white.

For a long moment Longarm gazed at the multicolored spectacle that spread as far as he could see. Then he broke the spell, saying aloud, "It's a right pretty sight, old son, but you wasn't sent here to gawk at a bunch of sand and rocks. And you ain't got a month to set around, either." Touching the horse with his boot-toe, he started the animal moving ahead.

As the morning wore on the air grew warm, then hot. Longarm let the horse set its own pace, touching the reins only when it was necessary to keep on the trail that was so seldom travelled that its lightly marked course was at times almost invisible.

Noontime came. He saw no real shade anywhere ahead or to either side in the sun-baked, treeless land, so he looked for and found a thin slice of half-shade under the overhang of a shelving mesa. He ate part of the perishable summer sausage he'd bought, and several of the flour tortillas with a slice of onion to give his scanty ration moisture and flavor. Washing down the meal with a carefully limited sip of water, he lighted a cheroot and set out on the trail once more.

He'd been riding for almost an hour after lunch when his instinct as well as his keen senses told him that he was being followed. Without being too obvious, he began watching his back-trail. He glanced behind him now and then for a few seconds, and twice in the next hour or so he made an unnecessary stop to rest the horse while he listened for any alien noise breaking the desert silence. Though he saw nothing to confirm his suspicions, the uneasy feeling persisted, for during two of his stops he'd heard what he was sure was the brief scuffling of a horse's hooves on the baked ground.

Longarm had learned an old Comanche trick years before, and he used it now. He scanned the terrain ahead more closely than usual until he spotted a small, isolated mesa with a base eroded by time and the weather into a series of deep crevices. Then, with a touch lighter than a feather's fall, and so imperceptibly that its reduced pace would not be noticed at once by a rider following him, he slowed the dun gelding he was riding until the base of the mesa was less than a hundred yards ahead.

Loosing a staccato yell, he suddenly dug his heels into the gelding's flanks and slapped the reins. The horse broke into a gallop. Reaching the mesa, Longarm reined his mount sharply toward the seamed base of the flat-topped rise and started around it.

At the first crevice he saw that was wide and deep enough to accommodate the horse, he yanked back hard on the reins. The dun dug in its hooves and stopped. Longarm turned it and rode into the shallow crevice. It was barely wide enough inside for him to turn the horse so that he was facing the opening, but he managed to wheel the animal around. Whipping his Winchester from its saddle scabbard, Longarm waited.

He did not have long to wait. Thudding hoofbeats broke the air only a few minutes after he'd reached the concealment of the crevice. The hoofbeats grew louder as the rider who'd been following him approached his hiding place. Longarm got a glimpse of the wide shoulders and brown face of a man leaning forward on the back of his racing horse as the rider flashed past the cleft. His look was too brief and fleeting for him to be sure of anything except that the man who had been dogging his trail was an Indian.

Longarm toed the dun sharply and rode out of the crevice behind the other horseman. The man was ahead of him now, and was not aware of Longarm's pursuit for several moments, until the two had covered the better part of half a mile. Then the Indian looked back. Longarm raised his Winchester to point to the sky and fired a shot into the air. He dropped the muzzle at once, the Winchester now covering the rider in front of him. The Indian pulled up, skidding his pony to a stop. He turned the animal and held it on a tight rein, waiting for Longarm's approach.

Before Longarm was within easy speaking distance, the Indian raised his right hand and extended it palm outward toward Longarm in the universal sign of peace. Longarm was certain that the Indian was a Navajo. He wore an uncreased black hat with a straight brim, a maroon jacket cinched at the waist by the wide belt that supported his pistol holster, and trousers of coarse, undyed duck. Instead of shoes or boots he wore sandals. The pistol holstered at his hip was an old nickel-plated First Model Smith & Wesson .32 and his saddle scabbard held a Spencer carbine.

With the distance between them diminishing, Longarm could see that the rider's hair was cut evenly around in a kind of bob that ended at his jawline. He did not have the hawk nose common to the Plains tribes. His nose was flat and had wide nostrils, and his eyes were more almond-shaped than round. He could have been any age from twenty to forty. Longarm guessed he was closer to the former.

Lowering the muzzle of his Winchester, Longarm returned the peace sign. He pulled up the dun half a dozen yards from the Navajo. When the Indian did not speak first, Longarm asked him, "You mind telling me why you been dogging my trail?"

In almost unaccented English the Indian replied levelly, "My instructions were to observe you from a distance, Marshal Long."

Concealing his surprise not only that the man should be speaking English almost flawlessly, but that he'd called him by name, Longarm asked, "And whoever gave you them orders, did they tell you to backshoot me when we got someplace where it'd be easy to tuck my body away so nobody could find it?"

"No. I was ordered to stop and identify myself if you discovered that I was following you." While he was speaking he had tugged at a rawhide thong around his throat, and pulled from the neck of his jacket a circlet of horsehide which had a silver medallion attached to its face. "My name is Tosih Nez. I am a member of the Navajo Police."

With something of a shock, Longarm realized that the man he was facing had jurisdiction equal to his own as long as they were on the Navajo Reservation. "Who told you to follow me?" he asked Tosih Nez.

"My orders were given to me by the Navajo council of elders. They are the government of our people and make the laws and rules on our lands."

"You got any more instructions I should know about?"

"Only to help you in any way I can, and to see that you get into no trouble and come to no harm while you are on the lands that belong to our tribe."

Longarm could not be quite sure, but he thought he detected amusement in the Navajo's voice. He asked, "Did your elders give you any reason why they wanted you to follow me?"

"My situation is like yours, Marshal Long," the Navajo replied. "I do not question my orders. I only obey them."

"Seems like you know a lot more'n I do," Longarm observed. "I guess you know why I was sent here."

"Yes. We know that you are not what we call *hatini*. That is the name we give to high officials from Washington who have more power than we do over the life we live."

"That'd mean the Indian Bureau?"

Tosih Nez nodded. "We know you have been sent to find truths that we have not been able to discover for ourselves about the way in which two of our *hatalih* died, and who is responsible. We want to know those truths as much as the men in the Indian Bureau do."

"I guess if you know that much, you got the whole layout covered," Longarm said. Tosih Nez made no reply, and the lawman continued, "Well, now that I found out you've been tailing me, we might as well ride on together. You know where I'm heading, and you know the country better than I do, so maybe you can save me some time and a lot of trouble. That all right with you?"

"It is what I hoped you would say, Marshal Long."

"Let's move along, then, Tosih Nez. I'd a lot sooner have you riding with me than in back of me."

"Since you have made the offer for me to ride beside you, I will not say no," the Navajo said soberly. "And because you are said to have great skill in the kind of work we share, it may be that I can also learn from you, Marshal Long."

They set their horses moving and Longarm said to the Navajo, "If we're going to ride together, I guess I better tell you that I don't set much store by titles and such. My friends call me Longarm."

"Do you consider me your friend, then? You did not know me when the day began."

"Well, if you ain't a friend, Tosih Nez, at least you ain't an enemy, or I'd imagine you'd've had plenty of chances to backshoot me. You must've started tagging along behind me a pretty good piece back."

"I have watched you since you left Winslow," Tosih Nez admitted. "Even though I had no authority to do this until we came onto Navajo land."

"I guess you know I have at least as much jurisdiction on your reservation as you have, don't you?" Longarm asked as they rode around the mesa to pick up the trail north. "Even if this is Navajo territory, it's still Federal land. My chief reminded me of that when he gave me this job to do."

"This is known also to our *hatalih*. They told me much the same thing. We do not dispute your authority, Mar— Longarm."

"That's good. But what about when we go onto the Hopi Reservation? Ain't your people got a treaty or something with them that you won't trespass on each other's land?"

Tosih Nez nodded soberly. "There is such an agreement. But it is that we *Dineh* will not enter Hopi land, and they will not enter our land in a hostile way, with war parties. We go to their villages and they come to our *hogans* alone or in small groups to trade. And we of the police may follow fugitives on Hopi land. The elders talked of this, too, when they decided that I should watch you."

"Then I guess we don't have anything to worry about." Longarm fished a cheroot out of his pocket and lighted it.

45

"We'll just cut a shuck for where the dead men were found, and see what kind of trail we can pick up that might give us a few of the answers we're looking for."

Chapter 6

Longarm tilted the canteen to his lips and took a scant swallow. The sun-warmed water wet his throat but did not really satisfy his thirst. He passed the canteen to Tosih Nez, then hunkered back on his heels and touched a match to the cheroot he'd been holding unlighted between his fingers.

"I got to say, it takes a hell of a long time to get from here to there on this reservation of yours," he told his companion. "If it'd been me, I'd've just cut a shuck straight up to where I was headed, instead of going all the way around like we been doing."

"Perhaps. But you would have gone to bed thirsty, and your horse as it grew weaker would have gone so slowly that the number of days spent in your journey would have been the same," the Indian replied.

Longarm and the Navajo policeman had been almost two days on the trail now, after leaving the spot where they'd met. Tosih Nez had insisted that they circle around the southern border of the Hopi Reservation instead of going through it, as Longarm had planned. He did not want to trespass on the Hopis' land, the Navajo had explained, because at this time of the year the Hopi people did not stay as close as usual to their homes and fields. Parties would be out collecting rattlesnakes for the annual snake dance and travelling to the pueblo where the dance would soon be held.

They'd ridden west and made a dry camp for the night in a small draw that cut through the barren, waterless expanse. That morning they'd started at daybreak, and now, with the sun about ready to disappear, had stopped well into the rough broken country just inside the edge of the Painted Desert.

"I ain't complaining, you understand," Longarm said. "Now that you've told me about the Hopis getting ready for that snake dance they're getting ready to have, I can see it just makes good sense to stay out of their way as much as we can."

"It is a bad thing for Navajos to meet Hopi snake-collecting parties," Tosih Nez said thoughtfully. "They are a suspicious people, and they would think I am a spy sent to learn the sacred secrets of their tribe."

"Would they feel the same way about me?"

Tosih Nez nodded. "Of course. Just as we *Dineh* would feel about you watching us make the sand symbols which were given us by the *Tse'ghi*."

"There's things about Indian religion I just can't figure out," Longarm told the Navajo. "Now, I ain't much of a psalm singer myself, but I don't know of any church where the pastor wouldn't invite me in for a service."

"I have not understood why it is that your holy men do this. While I attended the church school it was hard for me to separate what they called education from what they called religion."

"I've been wondering how you learned to talk English so well. Where was this school you went to?"

"In Gallup. The school, I think, was to be a small part of the church, but when even as children we refused to give up the belief in our *Yei,* it grew to be a real school."

"*Yei?* That'd be your gods or something like that?"

"Something like that," Tosih Nez agreed, in a tone that told Longarm he did not want to discuss the subject. They rode in silence for a few moments. Then the Navajo said, "You will excuse me if I do not explain to you more fully, Longarm. We of the *Dineh* do not discuss our religion as your people do."

"That's just one of the ways we're different, I guess."

"Very different," Tosih Nez agreed. "Now, I can understand, even if you do not, why the Hopi allow only their

48

own people to go near the *kiva* where the snakes are kept before the dance."

"You've never seen one of these snake dances, then?" Longarm asked.

Tosih Nez shook his head. "Few of my people have. And even fewer of yours, I think. You have perhaps heard that the Hopi are not warriors?"

"I heard the Navajos almost always came out on top when they had a fight with 'em."

"This is true. They fight very badly. Only once in the days when our people made war against them did the Hopi kill a full Navajo war party. It was many years ago. Our war party attacked their big pueblo on the Third Mesa while they were having the Snake Dance."

"It'd seem to me that was a good time to hit 'em—while they weren't looking for you," Longarm observed.

"It seemed so to our war chiefs, but they were wrong. And, soon after that, the Hopi moved their Snake Dance from the Third Mesa, between the mountain they call Zihi-dush-jihini and their sacred Black Mesa. Now the dance is held at the *kiva* in the place they call Tonalca, far to the north on their lands."

"Ain't that close to where we're heading?"

"Not close enough for us to worry. It is a long day's ride from the places where our *hatalih* died to the *kiva* where the Hopi now dance."

"How much longer is it going to take us to get where we're headed for?" Longarm asked.

"Four days, perhaps five. We cannot start north yet. We must keep moving west tomorrow, to the river you call the Little Colorado. It is the only place close by where we can be sure of finding good water."

Longarm knew from past experience the importance of water to men and their horses in land such as this. He realized that Tosih Nez was right in wishing to make sure that they had enough water for their trip, even at the expense of half a day's time. In the desert, the heat of the constantly beating sun was their greatest enemy.

"Can we carry enough water in my canteen and your water bag to get us where we're going without leaving the trail again?" he asked the Navajo policeman.

"If we are careful to keep the horses strong. When we reach the Moenkopi Wash as we go north, the water standing in its deep holes may still be sweet enough to drink. If it is not, and the horses begin to suffer, we will be near enough to the river to reach it in half a day."

"Sounds like we ain't really hit the rough part yet."

"There are many miles of bad travelling before we get to the place we go to. Above Moenkopi Wash, we must cross great sand dunes for two full days and part of another day."

"Well, a couple of days don't sound too bad."

"You will not say that when we start to cross. The dunes are so soft that even a riderless horse stepping on them sinks to its knee joints. And underneath, the sand is always hot. Snow melts when it falls on the dunes in the winter."

"Ain't there a way to go around the sandy place?" Longarm asked.

Tosih Nez shook his head. "Not a good way. On the east the sands reach to Tonalea, where the Hopi will be gathering. To circle the dunes by going west would take us three more days."

"Looks like we'll just have to go across 'em, then. But I don't aim to worry about the sand dunes till I see 'em." Longarm glanced at the western sky, redder now than the brightest rocks of the Painted Desert around them. "Right now I'm ready to spread my blanket out, and roll up in it, and go to sleep."

"I should have provided a Navajo pony for you," Tosih Nez told Longarm. The Navajo had not dismounted, but Longarm was standing beside the horse loaned him by the Indian Bureau. The animal stood with its sides heaving, swaying back and forth in the knee-deep sand, refusing to move.

"He sure ain't the best nag I ever forked," Longarm said. "We're just going to have to let him rest a little longer before we can start again."

"If he stands too long in the sun without moving he will die," Tosih Nez said. "If he does not move, he will not sweat. Without sweat to cool his body, the horse will soon

50

die unless he is given much water."

"We damn sure can't spare any more water for him, not if we ain't past the middle of these damned sand dunes yet, with a long ways to go ahead of us."

"But that is where we are," the Navajo pointed out. "And if we do not start soon, we will run out of water for our own use before we get through them."

Tosih Nez glanced at the sky, and Longarm followed suit. The sun was at its zenith, and its rays reflected from the seemingly endless expanse of sand had already raised the air to oven heat. Both men had long ago stopped sweating, though in the armpits of Longarm's shirt and Tosih Nez's jacket thin dark lines crusted white at the edges showed they were not yet dehydrated.

Even the brief upward glance he'd ventured had been enough to dry out Longarm's eyes, though. When he lowered his head and blinked, his eyelids grated like sandpaper over the sensitive pupils.

Longarm did not even suggest that they ride double and lead the weakening dun. Tosih Nez's pony was small, and he had seen how difficult it was for the pony to carry even one rider through the yielding sand. He said, "The only thing I can think of is for you to take my canteen and your water skin and ride to the river while I wait here with the horse."

"That is not possible, Longarm. To travel to the river and back from where we stand now would take three days. You and the horse would both be dead before I returned."

"We sure can't get this critter to move. Except, if we had some way to hitch your pony to him, we might be able to pull him along a step or two, get him started."

"Even if we had rope, which we do not, my horse has never pulled, Longarm. He was trained to be ridden."

"What if we used our reins? Tie 'em together—"

"I have no reins," Tosih Nez reminded him.

Longarm had forgotten that Tosih Nez rode Navajo-style. Instead of a saddle he had a pad of folded leather. For reins, the Navajo used a bitless rope headstall of braided horsehair with a short loop of the same kind of rope taking the place of long leather reins.

51

"Besides that," the Navajo went on, "even if we buckled the reins from your horse together to make a long enough strap, it would break under the strain of pulling."

"I already figured out that a single rein ain't going to be strong enough to haul this crowbait out of the sand if the damn fool animal just stands here like it is now. But if he saw another horse in front of him and got even a little bit of a tug, the brute might decide to start moving again."

"You may be right, Longarm. We can try."

Tosih Nez dismounted. His feet, like Longarm's, sank to the ankles in the treacherous sand, and he did not have boots to protect them, only sandals. He led his pony to the head of Longarm's mount and then stopped short.

Longarm had moved to the neck of the Bureau horse and was unbuckling the reins from the headstall. He said, "If worse comes to worst, I can hang onto your stirrup. No, damn it, you ain't got stirrups, either! All I can see, if this pulling don't work, is to leave the damned nag here to rot. And I'll walk the rest of the way!"

Tosih Nez made no reply. Longarm looked around when he got no response. The Navajo was standing with his arms raised, his head turned to the sky. Longarm's first thought was that his companion was praying, but he wasn't sure whether or not Navajos prayed in that fashion. Nevertheless, he stood silent until Tosih Nez lowered his head and opened his eyes.

"I must ask you something, Longarm," the Navajo said. "If it offends you, I am sorry."

There was a note in Tosih Nez's voice that sobered Longarm, and he said quietly, "Go ahead. Whatever it is, I guarantee I won't get angry."

"Is your word like that of some white men? Given quickly and broken as fast?"

Longarm's jaw dropped. It took him a moment to frame a reply. Then he said, "That's a hell of a question to ask a man."

"Yes," Tosih Nez agreed. "But we of The People have taken the word of too many of your people and have found their promises to be false. I ask you the question seriously, Longarm, and with a reason."

"I ain't one to brag—" Longarm began.

"This is a thing I have noticed since we have been riding together. And I am sure I know the answer to my question, but I must hear it from your lips."

"All I got to say is this. If I tell a man I'm going to do something, I'll do it—or die trying to."

"Then will you say to me that you will speak no word of what I am going to do?"

"I won't breathe a word to nobody, and that's a promise!"

"Very good. Leave the reins as they are, then."

Without understanding what was happening, Longarm stepped away from the horse's head. Tosih Nez struggled through the shifting sands to his own pony. He removed his sash and pulled his jacket off, then lifted the pony's saddle-pad and stroked his hands in the small, foamy puddle of sweat that had accumulated under the pad. He put his palms into his armpits and mixed the sweat with his own sweat. Then he spoke to Longarm.

"From this moment, you will promise to say nothing of what I do or what you see. On this I must have your word."

"You got it, Tosih Nez."

"It is good. Now take my horse and lead it to—" Tosih Nez pointed to a sand dune higher than those around it, about fifty yards distant. "Lead it to that dune."

Mystified, but sure that the Navajo had a reason for making the request, Longarm led the pony away. He'd covered about half the distance when he heard Tosih Nez begin to chant, and then he understood. The words and the atonality of Tosih Nez's voice were much like other Indian prayer chants Longarm had heard. He was careful not to look around until he reached the dune, but when he stopped there he stepped behind the pony and peered over its back.

Tosih Nez was standing with his bare head thrown back, the sun beating on his upturned face. His arms were extended upward and Longarm could hear faintly the chant that rose and fell in the thin air. The Navajo fell silent and stepped to the side of Longarm's dun. He lifted its saddle blanket and his hands disappeared briefly beneath it. When he removed his hands, Tosih Nez rubbed them in his armpits for a second time.

Stepping to the head of Longarm's mount, he rubbed his palms over the horse's nose. He spent several minutes doing this, his fingers reaching deep into the animal's nostrils. Resting his head against the dun's forehead when he took his hands away from its nose, Tosih Nez stood in that position for what to Longarm seemed a very long time. Then he stepped back and raised his arms once more and the strange, ragged rhythm of his chant again came faintly to Longarm's ears.

This time, the chant was short. Tosih Nez took the dun's reins and started walking ahead of the animal. When the leather straps tightened, the horse raised its head. Its muscles grew taut. It lifted a forefoot hesitantly, and put it forward. Then its haunches quivered and the dun freed itself from the sand and walked steadily behind Tosih Nez until the Navajo stopped.

Waving to Longarm, Tosih Nez shouted, "Come back now, Longarm. We can go on."

Longarm led the Navajo pony back to where Tosih Nez was standing beside the Bureau horse. The dun was quivering, but its head no longer sagged.

"Mount and ride," Tosih Nez told Longarm. "We have no time to waste."

Longarm swung into his saddle. Tosih Nez was already on his pony. Longarm followed him as the Navajo moved off, and pulled the dun up to ride abreast of his companion.

"You already got my word I ain't going to say nothing about what you just done," he told the Navajo policeman. "But I got a bump of curiosity right now that won't quit. Can you tell me what in hell you pulled off?"

Tosih Nez hesitated for a moment, then said, "With the help of the *Yei*, I have given your horse some of the strength I drew from my pony, and from my own body."

"But how'd you work it?" Longarm persisted.

"You saw what I did, but I cannot tell you how or why the prayers work. I was taught only what motions to make and the words of the prayer I offered to the *Yei*. There is a power in the mingling of sweat from my body and pony's body with that of your horse which has given it new strength and spirit. Truthfully, I was not sure that the prayer would be effective, with you looking on."

"Well, it sure worked. This nag's moving right along now, without acting a bit tired."

Tosih Nez only nodded. His shoulders were sagging and he was breathing deeply, as though exhausted. They rode on in silence. Preoccupied by what he'd just witnessed, Longarm did not notice for some time that Tosih Nez had started in a new direction. When he did, he frowned and turned to his companion.

"We're heading east, not north," he said. "I thought you didn't want to go onto the Hopi Reservation?"

"I did not. But it is the only thing we can do now. The nearest place where we can get fresh horses is the trading post at Shonto, and the quickest way to get there is to ride in a straight line."

"How come you're in such a hurry?"

"There will be many Hopi snake-collecting parties in the land we must cross now. We must travel swiftly while the horses can move well."

"Seems to me they're doing pretty good," Longarm said.

"They are. But the strength the prayer has given yours will not last long. They will carry us for a day, perhaps a bit longer. But we must get fresh horses as quickly as we can."

"We can always stop and give 'em a while to rest."

"Resting will not help them, Longarm. When the strength the *Yei* took from me and my pony is used up, your horse will die. And I cannot yet be sure, but my pony may die, too."

Chapter 7

Longarm stared at Tosih Nez. What he saw in the Navajo's face convinced him that his companion was serious. If he had not just seen the inexplicable transfusion of strength the Navajo had brought about in the dun, Longarm would have refused to believe it had happened. Now, he not only believed what he'd seen, but was prepared to accept as truth Tosih Nez's announcement that both animals might die as the result.

"Ain't there something else you can do to keep the horses alive?" he asked.

Tosih Nez shook his head. "The horses no longer belong to us, Longarm. In my prayers, I gave them to the *Yei*. If the *Yei* do not need them at once, we might be allowed to keep them a day or two longer, but very soon the *Yei* will claim what belongs to them. I have seen this thing before, you understand."

Longarm nodded. "If that's the way of it, then we had better make the best time we can."

They kept moving as fast as the soft clutching sand would allow them to, but sunset found them still plodding through the dunes. While on previous evenings Tosih Nez had always insisted on stopping at sundown, he did not do so now. They kept going under the scant light provided by the quarter-moon that limited their vision to a few hundred yards and, in spite of their eyes having adjusted to the darkness, revealed the sand dunes only as vaguely defined humps rising from mysterious black shadows.

56

As they moved slowly ahead, not even stopping from time to time to rest the horses, Longarm could feel the dun beginning to weaken. He wondered if Tosih Nez's pony was also flagging, but the two or three times Longarm had spoken to him after they'd resumed their journey, the Navajo had made only brief replies. Longarm decided to remain silent until his companion spoke to him.

Tosih Nez did not break his silence until the humps began to diminish in size and number and the sand became so shallow that the horses no longer had to struggle to lift their feet from it. Then he said quietly, "We are almost at the end of the sand. There is a water hole not far away. We will stop there."

Travelling over the hard soil after they left the dunes allowed them to speed their pace, even though the going was rougher. An hour dragged by after they'd reached solid ground, and most of another hour passed before the terrain began to slope downward and the baked earth to give way to a looser dirt that muffled the hoofbeats of their mounts. The tiring animals made somewhat better progress after they'd started on the downslope.

"When the horses begin to move faster than they are now, we must stop at once," Tosih Nez warned Longarm. "They will try to run when they smell water, and we must be sure that the water is still sweet before we drink it ourselves, or let them drink."

Only a few more minutes passed before the horses began to toss their heads. They snuffled and struggled to walk faster. Tosih Nez reined in his pony and slid off its back. He gave the animal a command in Navajo, and the pony stopped. Under his thighs, Longarm could feel the flanks of the dun beginning to quiver. Tosih Nez walked ahead, and Longarm's eyes, following him, made out the glint of water in the dark shadows in front of them.

In a moment, Tosih Nez called him. "We have luck, Longarm. The water is good. Bring your canteen and my water skin. We will fill them and drink before we let the horses come to the hole."

Though the water was brackish, it did not have the acrid taste of alkali in it. After the two men had drunk, they filled their containers and let the horses drink, pulling their heads up after they'd had their noses in the pool for a few moments at a time, until they were sure the animals would not founder by overfilling their stomachs suddenly.

Though they'd eaten only scantily during the long hot day, the two men did not feel hungry. Tosih Nez did not stop to tether his pony, but stretched out on his thick blanket as soon as the horses had been watered. Longarm dropped the reins of the dun to the ground and rolled a boulder over the leathers before turning in. He unsaddled the horse and carried his saddlebags and saddle a few feet away, to keep the animal from trampling on the gear during the night.

Even Longarm's iron frame was exhausted by the multiple strains he'd undergone during the past thirty-six hours. His eyes were drooping with fatigue and his muscles responded with reluctance to each movement his brain commanded them to make. He knew how tired he must be when he did not even take a nightcap of Tom Moore or light a final cheroot.

He slid his Winchester out of its saddle scabbard and laid the rifle beside his bedroll. Unbuckling his gunbelt, he put the holstered Colt where his hand could grab its butt without groping. Still wearing his boots and vest, he rolled up in his blanket and was asleep in thirty seconds.

Even exhaustion did not dull Longarm's finely honed senses. Not yet fully awake, he was reaching for the Winchester before he'd become consciously aware of the soft scraping noises that had disturbed him. Darkness still surrounded him, and Longarm's eyes did not immediately focus in the gloom after he'd snapped fully awake. He did not need to see anything to know that trouble had arrived when his hand found only earth where the stock of the rifle should have been.

Without an instant of wasted motion, Longarm's hand darted up to the butt of the Colt beside his head. Instead of grasping the wood and metal of the revolver's grip, his fingers closed on leather. It was not the firm polished leather of the Colt's holster, but the rough, soft-cured leather of a moccasin. There was a foot inside the moccasin, and it was holding the butt of the revolver hard against the ground.

Longarm started to sit up, but the cold muzzle of a rifle pressed hard on his forehead quickly changed his mind and he lay down again. Squinting, he rolled his eyes from one side to the other, and finally turned them upward. He saw the outline of a man standing over him, holding the rifle— Longarm's own Winchester—which was pinning him down. One of the captor's feet was planted on the Colt.

"Ka qouchata?" a strange voice called from where Tosih Nez had spread his blanket.

"Lo-lo—" the man holding Longarm captive began to say, when Tosih Nez interrupted.

"They're Hopi, Longarm. Do as they say."

"They got a gun on you, too?" Longarm asked.

"Yes."

If the Navajo had intended to say more, he had no chance. Longarm heard an angry voice raised in an unintelligible command, then the slap of flesh on flesh, and Tosih Nez was silent.

He understood why a moment later when a second Hopi appeared from the darkness. Without saying a word to the man who was holding the rifle, he bound Longarm's thumbs together with a strand of rawhide. Pulling down on the thong, he forced Longarm's hands flat, their palms together with the bound thumbs between them, his fingertips touching. He wrapped several spirals of the thong tightly around Longarm's hands and knotted the end.

Still without speaking, the Hopi grasped Longarm's chin and pulled it down. Before Longarm could move his head or close his jaws the Hopi had pushed a small wooden stick into his open mouth. Instinctively, Longarm bit down. With the same economy of motion he had used in binding Longarm's hands, the Hopi looped a second rawhide thong around the ends of the stick where they protruded from the sides of Longarm's mouth and secured it with a knot at the nape of Longarm's neck. Longarm tried to force the stick out with his tongue, but he was too late. The knots had already been tied.

Longarm tried to speak, but all that came from his mouth was a gargle of unmodulated sound. Seething with frustration, he had no choice but to allow the two Hopis to grab him by the elbows and swivel him around. Although he had not noticed until now, Longarm saw along the eastern horizon the first gray line of dawn.

Wan as the grayness was, it lessened the darkness enough for him to see the forms of three men between him and the water hole. As they came toward him and his captors, Longarm identified the man in the center of the trio as Tosih Nez. The Navajo policeman had been bound and gagged in the same fashion as Longarm.

Stopping when they came together, the four Hopis held a brief conversation, then one of the four left from the group and started running east, his figure outlined against the steadily brightening sky. The three remaining Hopis pushed Longarm and Tosih Nez to the ground. As soon as they were seated, two of the Hopis left the third one to watch their prisoners and went to the spot where Longarm had been sleeping. They piled his saddlebags and saddle into his blanket and pulled up the corners, tying them together to form a crude bag.

There was enough light now for Longarm to see the Hopis. He found little to distinguish them from the Navajo. Their noses were perhaps a bit more aquiline, their faces longer rather than square like the Navajo's, and their lips somewhat thinner. Instead of having their hair bobbed straight around their heads at the jawline, it was cut shorter, falling from their narrow headbands only to their earlobes.

They wore jackets similar in style to Tosih Nez's pullover, but their jackets, like their trousers, were of undyed cotton duck. Their moccasins were high, coming above their ankles, and they wore knee-high leggins made of the same thin sueded leather from which the moccasins were fashioned. Their bodies were stocky, but they moved easily as they worked at gathering up Longarm's gear.

When the three Hopis finished tying together the corners of Longarm's bedroll, the man who was standing guard turned his back on the captives to watch as they went to attend to Tosih Nez's possessions. Unobserved, Longarm began testing his bonds. He could do nothing about the gagging stick, so he concentrated on his hands. Each time he tried to force his palms apart, the leather thongs around his thumbs pulled the joints downward and sent pangs of pain shooting up his arms almost to his elbows.

Even when his thumbs grew numb, and Longarm could no longer feel them, his movements in trying to get a bit of play in the leather thong were so painful to his wrists and arms as to be intolerable. After a few more minutes of unrewarded effort, Longarm decided to stop torturing himself and wait.

Though little time had elapsed since the Hopis moved in on their camp, the sky had grown appreciably brighter. Longarm turned his head and found that he could now see Tosih Nez's features quite clearly. He raised his eyebrows, and the Navajo responded with a slight shrug. Longarm tried to read his eyes, but they were as opaque and expressionless as always.

Then Tosih Nez inclined his head toward the water hole. Longarm looked and saw the Navajo pony lying dead at its edge. In the swift pace of his capture, Longarm had not thought of his own horse until now. Turning his head, he saw it lying beside the boulder he'd used for a tether. The dun's head was thrown back at an awkward angle, its neck looking twice as long as it had when the horse was alive. A single glance was enough to tell Longarm that the dun was also dead.

Glancing around, Longarm saw that they were in a shallow valley. He supposed it was the Moenkopi Wash which he'd seen on his map, and which Tosih Nez had mentioned. He could see little of the surrounding terrain. The wash was a shallow arroyo with a gravel bottom. Beyond the water hole in the foreground, the gravel stretched to the opposite side, perhaps a quarter of a mile wide. The wash itself wound roughly from the northeast to the southwest. Its serpentine curves cut off the view in both those directions, and the rounded ridge at the top of the downslope hid everything except the mile or so of the bottom of the wash itself.

Paying no attention to their prisoners, the four Hopis hunkered down a few paces away from Longarm and Tosih Nez. They took thin flat rounds of bread from somewhere in their loose cotton jackets and began eating. Longarm was suddenly aware that he was ravenously hungry. He tried to swallow, but the stick that held his mouth open also pressed down on the back of his tongue, and each time he started the motion of swallowing, his tongue moved in reflex action and gagged him. He put his mind to forgetting his hunger, and when thirst replaced the hunger pangs, he suppressed his desire for water, too.

While the Hopis ate, the sun came up in a clear light-blue sky. After consuming their bread, the Hopis walked down to the water hole one by one to drink, still ignoring Longarm and Tosih Nez. The sun had turned from red to burnished brass before anything broke the monotony of the early morning.

Longarm heard the wagon creaking long before it came into sight on the lip of the long slope that led down to the water hole. The wagon was a four-wheeler, rickety and unpainted. Its axles began complaining even louder when the single horse that drew it stiffened its legs as it reached the final precipitous hundred yards where the ground dropped to the gravel bottom. The three Hopis who had been guarding Longarm and Tosih Nez got up and went to meet the wagon.

Its passengers were four Hopi men, three of them squeezed together on the seat and the fourth sitting in the wagonbed. The three men in the seat were dressed much like those who were guarding Longarm and Tosih Nez.

It was the man in the wagonbed who drew Longarm's attention. He had on a crimson sateen jacket with a wide blue sash, and a necklace made of triple strands of lump turquoise hung from his neck in loops that reached almost to his waist. His hair was worn long, falling over his shoulders and down his back. His face was much lighter than those of the other Hopis, and as the wagon creaked to a stop Longarm could see that the man's face had been smeared with some kind of yellow-white paste or powder.

While the three Hopi guards were walking to the wagon, the men on its seat alighted, and all the six of them clustered around the wagonbed and spoke to the man seated there. The distance was too great for Longarm to hear what they were saying, and he could not have understood their words in any event.

Tosih Nez had also turned as best he could to look at the wagon, and Longarm got his attention by shrugging his shoulders until the Navajo policeman turned back to look at him. Longarm tried to question his companion with his eyes, but Tosih Nez could only shake his head. Helplessly, the two prisoners watched the Hopis.

Whatever their discussion or argument was about, it lasted for only a few minutes. The man in the wagon got up and stepped over the seat and from there to the ground. The others were taking from the wagonbed square pieces of the same thin leather from which their leggins were made. They wrapped the squares around their waists like aprons.

One of them produced a wide-mouthed pottery jar from beneath the seat, and they smeared their faces with the yellow-white paste it contained. Reaching into the wagon-bed again, each of the Hopis took out two sticks, one of the sticks three or four feet long, slim and pointed, the other stick half that length, with a pair of eagle wing feathers bound to one end to form a narrow vee. Then each of them picked up a cotton sack from the bed of the wagon and the group scattered out along the sloping sides of the wash.

The red-jacketed man came up to where Longarm and Tosih Nez sat bound and gagged. The Hopi gazed for a moment at the two, then spoke to the Navajo. His voice was deep and resonant, but harsh. Longarm could not tell whether the newcomer was speaking in Hopi or Navajo— he had no knowledge of either language—but he deduced that the Hopi was asking Tosih Nez a question or perhaps several questions, for when the man stopped speaking, Tosih Nez nodded affirmatively. Another question followed, but this time the Navajo shook his head vehemently. The Hopi replied with a short, angry speech.

Planting a foot on Tosih Nez's shoulder, the Hopi pushed him flat on the ground. Longarm wondered if his turn was next and quickly got his answer, for the Hopi gave him the same treatment. Walking the short distance to the wagon, the Hopi returned with a pair of cotton sacks like those the others had taken with them, and tossed the sacks over the captives' heads.

Blinded now as well as bound and gagged, Longarm had no alternative but to lie quietly and wonder what the future held. He soon decided that there was little point in worrying, and concentrated again on trying to free himself. His hands were completely numb by now, but each time he willed himself to pull them apart, stabbing pains shot like tiny lightning bolts up his forearms and forced him to stop.

For a few minutes, Longarm lay still. Then he noticed that there was a tiny gap between the ground and the edge of the sack that was covering his head. He concentrated on widening the gap. Turning his head caused the stick-gag to grate against his teeth, but he ignored that. He twisted his neck again and again until he'd lifted the sack's edge almost two inches above the ground.

All that he could see at first was a stretch of the boulder-strewn gravel which lined the bottom of the wash. Then one of the Hopis came into sight. The man was running, his torso bent forward, the long stick in his left hand, the shorter wand with the feathers at its tip in his right.

While he ran, the Hopi moved the long switch from side to side along the ground. As he came closer and Longarm could see more clearly, he could make out the undulating brown streak of the rattlesnake the man was chasing. The snake suddenly took off in a new direction, and headed for the spot where Longarm and Tosih Nez were lying helpless.

Instinctively, in pure reflex action, Longarm moved his arms, reaching for the Colt he no longer wore. The pain his involuntary motion caused did not stop in his forearms this time, but ran up to his shoulders. Longarm forced himself to go limp. He lay quietly, only his eyes moving as the snake slithered toward him. A yard away, the rattler stopped. Hissing angrily, it reared and began coiling, getting ready to strike.

Chapter 8

Even though Longarm knew his face was hidden by the sack, he drew back involuntarily from the rattler writhing in front of him. The snake's body undulated over the rough ground as it began forming the coils from which it launched its deadly strike. Its rattles buzzed angrily, its tail vibrating faster than Longarm's eyes could follow. Then the Hopi came into his restricted field of vision. The man had his long stick extended, and began tapping at the rattler's body. The snake interrupted its sinuous coiling to rear up. It swung its head from side to side. Its forked tongue had been darting from its mouth incessantly, but now the tongue no longer showed.

Slowly, the Hopi stretched out the hand in which he held the feather-tipped wand. With wrist flicks that moved the wand's tip even faster than the snake could dart its head, he tapped the rattler's head, first on one side, then on the other. The rattler froze, its head rigidly erect, no longer swaying. The quick taps following one after the other on opposite sides of its head seemed to confuse the serpent.

Less than a yard separated the Hopi and the snake. The Hopi turned the feather-tipped wand horizontally and began stroking the snake's upreared head with the feathers. The triangular head started moving again, not rapidly this time, but swaying gently in a shallow arc. The Hopi lengthened the strokes of the wand and bit by bit the tension left the rattler's body. The buzzing of its rattles died away.

After a moment, the rattler lowered its head, and its body

slowly straightened out. The Hopi continued to stroke the snake's head for a few moments. Then he dropped his long wand, his hand shot forward, and he grasped the snake below its head. He lifted the reptile high, shook open the mouth of the sack that was hanging from his sash, and lowered the snake into the bag.

As the Hopi walked past his head in the direction of the wagon, Longarm could see that the rattler the man had just captured was not alone. The sagging heft, weight, and humping movements of the cloth sack's deep sides showed that it contained several more snakes.

Suddenly the sack covering Longarm's head was whisked away. He looked up. One of the Hopis was standing over him. The man's face was still covered with the white paste the Hopis had smeared on before starting their snake hunt. The man dragged Longarm to his feet. Being yanked up by the wrists put a sudden strain on Longarm's already sore arms, but he kept his face immobile in spite of the rush of pain.

A few yards away the Hopi who wore the red sateen jacket was standing and Longarm found himself being half-led, half-pulled to where he waited. While he'd been watching the activities around the wagon at the beginning of the snake hunt, Longarm had deduced that the man in red must be some sort of tribal leader. The man who was leading Longarm pulled him to a stop, and, at a nod from his leader, removed the stick-gag from Longarm's mouth.

"Hai-komi, quo-cha-ta?" the Hopi asked.

Longarm could guess the man was asking who he was, but he made no effort to reply. The treatment he and Tosih Nez had received from the Hopis did not dispose him to feel kindly toward their leader. He was well aware that he would lose face if he seemed in any way to propitiate the Hopi. Besides, he wanted to get an idea of how much, if any, English the man knew.

Without taking his eyes off the Hopi, Longarm worked his jaws a few times to relieve the cramping caused by the stick-gag. He swallowed the saliva that had begun flowing again when the gag was removed. Then he turned his head from side to side, not only to relieve the strained muscles in his neck, but to steal a glance at Tosih Nez. The Navajo policeman was still sitting on the ground, his gag in place. When Longarm again looked at the Hopi, he kept his face blank, as though he had not heard the man's question and was waiting for him to repeat it.

Impatiently now, the leader said, "You bring no good company here, *quo-cha-ta*. Say me why."

Ignoring the leader's growing frown, which was cracking the white paste with which his face was smeared, Longarm at last replied, "Where I come from, a man likes to know who's asking him questions before he answers any. I guess you got a name?"

Grudgingly, the Hopi man replied, "Esta-qua. With my people am *tu-hik-ya,* what you call medicine chief."

"My name's Long. With my people and yours, too, Esta-qua, I'm a United States Marshal. You know what that means?"

"Big law," the leader said.

Longarm went on, "If you know that much, you know that I've got as much right to be here as any Hopi has. Now, suppose you tell your man to untie my hands before we do any more talking."

Longarm didn't know whether his failure to be awed by his title angered the medicine chief, or whether the Hopi was simply angry with all whites as a matter of course. For whatever reason, Esta-qua's brows drew down into a scowl.

"Why you do bring *tuva-suh* on Hopi lands?" he demanded, pointing at Tosih Nez. "To spy on Hopi's sacred ways?"

"If you're talking about that Snake Dance you're getting ready to have, neither one of us gives a tinker's damn about it. We come here to find out about the two Navajos and the Indian Bureau man who were killed up here a little while back."

"Tuva-suh do not come welcome!" Esta-qua exclaimed angrily. "Enemies of Hopi! They say we kill their *wu-ya,* but we do not!"

"I ain't heard Tosih Nez say that," Longarm said, jerking

a thumb over his shoulder at the Navajo. "And I sure ain't said it myself. All we come for is to find out what happened."

Esta-qua stood and for several moments his eyes shifted from Longarm to Tosih Nez and back to Longarm. Finally he said, "You come with us to pueblo."

"I don't know as I care to, Esta-qua. We're heading north, up to the trading post at Shonto."

"How? Horses die." Esta-qua pointed to the bodies.

"Oh, I'd imagine we can get there one way or another."

Esta-qua pointed to Longarm's bound hands and gave a rasping laugh. "You like or no, you come."

Longarm had played too much poker not to know when a bluff was being called. He took his time replying, and when he did, he kept his voice casual. "All right, Esta-qua. We'll see what your council says when they've heard the whole story. Get your wagon ready, and we'll ride with you."

"You think they're ever going to let us out of this damn hole?" Longarm asked.

"They will take us out when they are ready," Tosih Nez answered resignedly.

"It wouldn't be much of a trick to bust out the boards in that door," Longarm said for the tenth time since they'd been confined in the tiny chamber. "Or the boards on the window, for that matter. They're both so full of cracks they're about to fall apart."

Their improvised prison was at the top level of one of the three-story adobe buildings that made up the pueblo of Tonalea. Like all Hopi pueblos, this one consisted of several individual structures grouped to enclose an open plaza. The room in which Longarm and Tosih Nez were confined was in the central structure of three which stood in a U-shaped open rectangle. In common with pueblo structures, this one had been built on three levels, each level stepped back from the one below it. Rooms on each level opened onto the roof of the lower level, and ladders on each level provided access to the one above.

"What good would it do us to break out, Longarm?" the

Navajo asked, just as he had before. "All of the Hopis on the reservation who belong to the Snake and Antelope clans are down in that plaza, or on top of one of these buildings, right now. Some of the young men might kill us just for being where outsiders are forbidden."

"I know, you keep telling me that," Longarm replied stubbornly. "But I ain't one who enjoys being locked up— not when I can do something about it. Why're we having to wait so long?"

"Right now the Hopi must feel we are a lot less important than getting ready for the final part of the dance. Tonight or tomorrow morning, the elders' council will meet and call for us."

"Damned if you don't sound just like that Esta-qua! And he is one man I have no use for!"

"I know," Tosih Nez said. "He has no use for us, either— me in particular. That is why I feel we must wait until we can talk to the whole Hopi council."

"I know you've got the right idea, Tosih Nez. I just keep thinking about all the time we're wasting, and getting edgier and edgier, because I don't like being shut away like we are."

"We will not have to wait much longer," Tosih Nez said. "They ought to begin the Snake Dance pretty soon, and the elders' council will meet when the dance is over. Most of them have a long way to go to get back to their own pueblos, and they will be wanting to start back."

Longarm walked over to the room's single window and put his eye to the widest crack in its board shutter. He could see most of the plaza through the crack. At one corner of the open end a ladder protruding from a hole led to the underground *kiva,* the sacred chamber where the dancers sang their prayer chants and donned their ceremonial garb before the dances.

Earlier, Longarm and Tosih Nez had watched a number of men wearing leggins and aprons similar to those worn by the snake gatherers who had captured them descend into the *kiva.* Soon after they had gone down the ladder, a lattice of boards had been laid across its entrance, and on the planks a head-high cylinder of fresh, green-leafed branches of juniper and fir and cottonwood had been assembled.

"What's that for?" Longarm had asked Tosih Nez.

"They call it a *kisi*," the Navajo replied. "All the snakes that will be used in the dance are in the *kiva* now, and the men who just went down the ladder will hand them up through those branches to the dancers."

"How do you know so much about the Hopis, you being a Navajo?"

"All I know is what I have heard from Navajos who have seen the dance. The Hopis do not welcome visitors to this dance, as I have told you, but some of our people have managed to watch it."

"Spying?" Longarm asked.

Tosih Nez grinned and shrugged. "There have been Hopis who spied on us making our sacred sand pictures. Why should we not watch Hopi secrets?"

A drumbeat started to sound rhythmically somewhere outside the plaza, beyond Longarm's restricted range of vision. Tosih Nez came over to join him at the window. "Good," he said. "The dance is beginning."

Led by the drummer, the dancers marched across the plaza in single file. Their faces were whitened and striped down the nose and cheeks with red lines. They wore feathers, not in any sort of stylized headdress, but stuck at odd angles into their hair. Over their shoulders, antelope skins were draped. Some of them carried gourd rattles, which they shook in time with the drumbeats. Their chant formed a counterpoint to the beat of the drums and rattles. They crossed to the open end of the plaza and formed a line between the two pueblo buildings that enclosed its sides.

"They the ones that'll do the dance?" Longarm asked.

"No. They're Antelope clan men. They just play the music. The Snake clan men do all the dancing."

"I wouldn't exactly call it music," Longarm said. "It all sounds strange to me."

"So would our Navajo songs—just as your music sounds odd to us."

Longarm did not reply. The drumming had taken on a new, faster tempo, and he was watching a line of Hopis enter the plaza. From Tosih Nez's remark, Longarm figured them to be the men of the Snake clan.

These new arrivals had blackened their faces, and wavy white lines had been traced on their cheeks as well as on the reddish-brown paint that covered their torsos. Some of them had painted their arms pink, others a brighter red than the paint covering their bodies. Longarm guessed that the wavy lines represented snakes, and was sure his guess was right when the line began to turn as it approached the *kisi* and he saw the same white lines on their arms and thighs. Their headdresses were eagle feathers arranged in the shape of a shallow inverted bowl.

As the file turned to form an oval in front of the *kisi*, he saw that they had coyote or desert fox skins dangling from the backs of their waistbands; some wore one skin, others two. Each of them carried one of the short eagle-feather-tipped wands he'd seen the snake gatherers use. When the last of the line had joined the oval in front of the *kisi*, the drumbeat changed for the second time, and the Snake clan men began to circle in a shuffling dance that seemed to have no connection with the beat of the drum and the rattles.

"I don't see any snakes," Longarm commented.

"You will in a minute or two," Tosih Nez answered.

Still holding to their oval formation, the dancers stamped back and forth across the plaza. They had begun a chant now, which grew steadily in volume as the dance progressed. Suddenly the drumbeat took on an even quicker pulse and the Antelope men added their voices to the chanting. The oval of dancing men started back across the plaza toward the *kisi*, but in the center of the open space the formation broke into groups of three.

Raising their knees higher now, the dancers added gyrations and body twists to what had been a slow-paced dance using only their feet. One of the trios shuffled into a line, the second dancer grasping the shoulder of the first, the man in the rear holding the shoulder of the man ahead of him. The three went in rhythmic step to the *kisi*. The first man plunged his hand into the branches and when he brought it out he was holding a writhing, squirming rattlesnake.

While Longarm's eyes followed the first dancer in the group, the second man also received a snake from the *kisi*, and the trio headed across the plaza, waving the snakes at arm's length and raising them high in the air. Following them with his eyes, Longarm saw now that except for half a dozen men the entire formation had broken up into groups of three. Each group danced past the *kisi*, and the first two men each received a snake.

Without taking his eyes off the plaza, Longarm asked Tosih Nez, "How come there's three men and only the first two get snakes?"

"You would have to ask a Hopi that. And I don't think they could tell you—or would tell you if they could."

Both men were staring through the slit boards at the plaza, which was now filled with trios brandishing rattlesnakes as the dancers gyrated in no sort of order, crisscrossing and sometimes nearly colliding.

Suddenly Longarm was aware that some of the groups of three now had a snake for each man. He watched more closely, and saw that while they danced the men were handing the snakes to one another and swinging past the *kisi* for a second time, when the first man would get a fresh snake. Then he noticed that the third man in some of the trios was holding one or more snakes in each hand, and understood why the man in the rear had not been given a rattler on the trio's first visit to the *kisi*. He pointed this out to Tosih Nez.

"Yes, I noticed that. But the dance will soon be over, I think. There seem to be no more snakes being handed out as the dancers go past the *kisi*."

One of the Snake clan men from the group which had not taken part in the dance left the others standing near the *kisi* and began dancing among the trios still crisscrossing the plaza. He carried a pouch, and from it he dusted the dancers with some kind of fine whitish powder as he passed them.

"You got any idea what that is he's dusting 'em with?" Longarm asked, keeping his eyes at the crack in the shutter.

"Cornmeal, I believe. The Hopis are farmers, they have enough to waste. We Navajos grow little corn, so we must eat all of ours."

A second man left the hitherto idle group and began outlining a large circle in the plaza's center with some of the same kind of white powder the first man was sprinkling on the dancers. The first pouch-bearer came to join him. The chanting grew even louder. The dancing trios started moving around the circle that had been scratched in the dirt.

After dancing around its circumference several times, the dancers began tossing their snakes on the ground inside the circle. As their hands emptied, they kept dancing, but now they used their feather-tipped wands to keep the snakes from leaving the circle.

"Don't any of them dancing fellows ever get snakebit?" Longarm frowned.

"I am told they do, but the bites do not seem to harm them."

"I guess they know something about snakes the rest of us still ain't learned, then."

"Perhaps. Or perhaps it is their *Yei* who keep them from harm."

Two women bearing a large basket between them shuffled up to the snake-filled circle and emptied the basket over the snakes that were heaped in a wriggling mass inside it. They spat on the snake several times before retreating.

Their spitting was evidently a sign that the dance had ended, for now the Antelope clan men quit their chant and ran to join the Snake clan dancers in spitting on the snakes. The dancers were not watching the reptiles closely now, and some of the rattlesnakes escaped from the circle and started weaving across the plaza. Always there was a dancer ready to pick up the snake hurriedly and toss it back with the others.

A single drumbeat sounded. The Antelope clan men retreated from the circle, and the Snake clan men plunged as a group into the heap of squirming rattlers. They picked them up, some of them grabbing two or three snakes in each hand, and scattered across the plaza. They were quickly out of the range of vision of Longarm and Tosih Nez.

Longarm reached into his vest pocket for a cheroot before he remembered that he had none. "What'll they do with the snakes now?" he asked.

"Take them to where they found them and set them free."

"After all the trouble they went to, catching 'em and

carrying 'em here, they just let 'em go?"

"Wasn't it enough?" Tosih Nez asked. Then he added, "The Hopis went to some trouble to catch us and carry us here. They will be coming to take us before their elders soon, I would guess. Let us hope that we are as lucky as the snakes."

Chapter 9

Tonalea's council chamber had been intended to accommodate only the pueblo's own handful of elders. Since the *wu-ya* of the entire Hopi nation were on hand for the Snake Dance, all had been invited to sit in judgement on Longarm and Tosih Nez. The visiting elders, from Jeddito and Toreva in the reservation's southeastern corner to Kawaiokuh, Walpai, Shongopovi, Oraibi, Bacobi and Sichimovi in the center, crowded the room and made it uncomfortably warm.

Longarm looked at the faces of the Hopi elders while he waited for the council to begin. The single lantern that hung from a *viga* in the center of the room's low ceiling lighted the bronze faces of the men in the two front rows, but there were three more rows behind them, and the uncertain shadows hid more of the men sitting in them than the yellowish light revealed.

Among the twenty or so men packed into the small chamber, not more than three or four were young. Most of the faces of the council members were seamed and fissured, like the surface of the land in which the Hopis lived. Still, in spite of their age, a majority of the faces of the men gathered bore vestiges of either the black paint worn by the Snake clan or the white paste that the men of the Antelope clan had put on, indicating they had taken part in the dance two or three hours ago.

Aside from looking at him curiously when he was brought into the room, the Hopis paid little attention to Longarm. Though none of them had made any effort to talk with him, they treated him more as a guest than as a prisoner. One of the council members had dismissed the two guards that brought him in, but Longarm had a feeling that the two husky young men were close at hand, probably just outside the door.

Looking at the impassive faces around him, Longarm wished that he had a cheroot or two, but his coat and saddlebags had not been returned to him. Even more than wishing for a cigar, he wished that Tosih Nez was with him to pick up some of the low-voiced conversation that was going on among the council members and tell him what they were saying.

Longarm and Tosih Nez had just finished their supper— small flat loaves of *pika* bread with a stew of lamb and corn which the Navajo said was called *kun-kivi*—when two young Hopi men had come to take Longarm to the council room. They had shoved Tosih Nez aside unceremoniously as he started for the door to go along. Tosih Nez had argued with them—Longarm could not tell whether they'd spoken Hopi or Navajo, since both sounded equally strange to him—but the guards refused to let the Navajo policeman join Longarm.

"You must go alone," Tosih Nez finally said. "Perhaps it will be better if you do. The council won't feel that you are their enemy. The Hopi don't especially like your people, but they hate mine."

"I got a hunch they feel about the same towards both of us. These Hopis sure ain't treated me like I'd expect 'em to treat one of their friends."

"Only Esta-qua thinks of you as an enemy, Longarm. You did not show respect for his position as a *tu-hik-ya*. He will speak against you, but it is the council that will decide."

"Now, damn it, Tosih Nez, it stands to reason they're going to listen to that Esta-qua instead of me. And he never made no bones about being real hostile."

"That is because you and I were together. The worst he can tell the council is that you brought me onto their reservation, where I'm not supposed to be."

"How in hell do they expect me to understand what he's

telling 'em, or what they're talking about amongst themselves?" Longarm had objected.

"All of them speak English," Tosih Nez had assured him. "Some of the old ones understand it better than they speak it, though. And none of them really likes to speak anything but Hopi."

"Well, it don't look like we got much choice. I'll do the best I can."

A stirring of motion at the door of the council chamber drew Longarm's attention. Esta-qua, whom he hadn't seen since their arrival at the pueblo in midafternoon, was weaving his way through the room to the small cleared space in the center where Longarm stood. Like the faces of so many of the men already in the room, Esta-qua's face bore a few black smudges left from the paint that had covered it during the dance.

Ignoring Longarm, the *tu-hik-ya* pushed himself into the front row of the elders. The men already sitting in the row squeezed together politely to make room for him. Longarm noticed, if the other Hopis in the room did not, that Esta-qua chose a position as far from Longarm as he could get in the restricted space available.

In his boyhood, Longarm had once been taken to a Quaker meeting, where no one was in charge and anyone rose to speak when the spirit moved them. The assembly of Hopi elders reminded him of that. None of the elders seemed to be in charge of the council. For the most part, they sat motionless, though now and then one would exchange a few words with the man sitting next to him.

Longarm found himself wishing for a volunteer to stand up and start the proceedings, and he was relieved when one finally did, even though it was Esta-qua. The medicine man rose and looked around the room, then spoke briefly in Hopi. Two or three times during the short talk, the eyes of the elders turned to Longarm, but he could not tell from the impassive faces what the men were thinking.

Old son, Longarm told himself, *you better find out just exactly what this meeting's all about. There ain't nobody going to tell you unless you ask, and that son of a bitch Esta-qua is most likely spinning some fancy yarn that he's made up in his own head about what you and Tosih Nez done to him.*

When Esta-qua had finished talking, Longarm waited what he considered to be a decent interval, allowing time for any of the elders to take the floor. Then he stood up.

"Now, I don't know how many of you men understand what I'm saying," he began. "Maybe you don't understand English any more than I do Hopi. Fact of the matter is, I ain't sure why I was brought here to start with. My name's Long, and I guess you know I'm a Deputy U. S. Marshal. Now, seeing as all of you are in charge of the whole Hopi tribe, you're bound to know that I've got as good a right to be here as any of you have." He stopped and looked at the expressionless faces surrounding him, and asked, "Do you understand what I been saying?"

"We understand, Long," one of the seam-faced elders in the back row replied. "When we do not, we will stop you and ask you to be more plain."

Longarm nodded his thanks. "Now, I ain't got no idea what that man—" he pointed at Esta-qua—"has told you I done. But what happened was that yesterday morning him and some of your snake gatherers run across me and a Navajo policeman who was with me. Now, we knew about the treaty you Hopi folks got with the Navajos, about keeping off each other's land—"

One of the men in the front row spoke before Longarm could continue. "You know about our law, why do you break it?"

"We didn't start out to," Longarm replied. "We'd had a mite of trouble with our horses. Matter of fact, both of 'em died while we were asleep. The reason we were on your reservation is because when the horses began to weaken, we knew we had to cut a shuck in a straight line to get to the trading post up at Shonto, so we took the shortest route."

Esta-qua jumped up. Raising his voice to override Longarm's, he said, *"Haliksa-i! Um hak—"*

"No, Esta-qua!" one of the elders across the room and behind Longarm interrupted. "Speak with the tongue of the man you accuse! Marshal Long must hear what you say of him!"

For a moment, Esta-qua was silent, his jaw clenched angrily. Then he went on, "I do what you ask, Sa-ka-mosi."

Longarm had turned away from the medicine man to look at the one who had spoken, and when he faced Esta-qua again he read pure hatred in the Hopi's eyes.

Esta-qua went on, "My brothers, do not let this Long lie to you! He had with him *tuva-suh*! Why you think? We have our dance most sacred to Hopi! *Tuva-suh* is come to spy!"

"Now, that ain't the truth, and you know it," Longarm said quickly.

Another of the elders interrupted. "Let Esta-qua speak!"

"I ain't trying to stop him," Longarm told the man. "Only he's talking about somebody that ain't here to talk back. Tosih Nez wasn't spying. He's a Navajo policeman, and he was with me on a case. Get him down here and let him speak for himself."

One of the elders called out, *"Lo-loma! Lo-loma!"*

"Na! Tuva-suh nukpana!" someone behind Longarm countered.

In the space of a few seconds the council room became a riot of voices as the Hopi elders argued among themselves over the question of bringing a hated Navajo into their council chamber.

Longarm did not understand exactly what was being said, but he knew that he'd touched off the argument with his suggestion. Esta-qua knew it, too, and during the moments when he was not contributing to the confusion of voices, the medicine man glared angrily at Longarm.

As the heated discussion continued, Longarm tried to guess which side was going to win the dispute, but as far as he could tell, the council was about equally divided. Gradually, the exchanges between the disputants grew calmer and less protracted. A few die-hards on each side of the argument kept it going for a while after the first flurry subsided, but when one of the elders silenced the few who still persisted by pounding the floor with the cane which

79

represented the elders' authority, then began to flourish the stick in the air, the voices were finally hushed.

Waving the polished black cane in the air, the elder said loudly, "We act like children! Honor the *mong-ko* we carry!" He waved the cane above his head again to emphasize his point and went on, "Why do we fear one *tuva-suh?* Esta-qua is wrong, and Long is right. Bring the *tuva-suh* here and let him speak!"

When the elders began to argue again, Longarm could see clearly that the majority favored listening to Tosih Nez. He glanced at Esta-qua. The medicine man had seen, as had Longarm, that he had failed to persuade the council to condemn the Navajo out of hand. The corners of his mouth were drawn down in disgust and, as he turned to look at Longarm, his eyes slitted angrily.

You better keep an eye on that buzzard, old son, Longarm cautioned himself. *He's been out to make trouble from the start, and he ain't changing his mind none. Trouble is, there ain't much you can do right now, because you ain't got a hell of a lot to work with.*

One of the elders in the front row got up to leave the room. Longarm frowned, but before he could look around to see if any others were getting ready to depart, the man returned. He wove through the rows until he reached the cleared spot in the center of the room and held up his hand.

"We will hear the Navajo. I have sent the guard to bring him here," he announced.

If there were any grumbles from the other elders, Longarm did not hear them. The Hopis began talking among themselves. He noticed that only one of the men closest to Esta-qua had anything to say to the medicine man.

Tosih Nez arrived. The elders between the center of the room and the door opened a path for him to go and take his place beside Longarm.

"What did you say to make these Hopis agree to listen to a Navajo?" he asked, while they waited for the council chamber to grow quiet again.

"It wasn't me." Longarm pointed to the elder who'd been so insistent that Tosih Nez be present. "It was that fellow there that did the real talking. All I did was remind 'em you weren't here to speak for yourself."

"Has the *tu-hik-ya* told them yet that I came to spy?"

"He said something to that effect."

"What have you told them?"

"Nothing but the bare bones. None of 'em asked where we were heading or why."

Longarm stopped talking when the elder who'd been so largely responsible for persuading the council to hear Tosih Nez stood up and said, gazing at the Navajo as he spoke, "I am Mumu-ri-wu."

"I am Tosih Nez. The Navajo Council has honored me by making me one who sees that all obey our people's laws."

"Then why do you break Hopi law?" Esta-qua asked loudly.

Before anyone else could speak, Tosih Nez replied, "It was to help the Hopi people that Marshal Long and I were travelling. We did not have time to waste. We were not coming to Tonalea. We took the shortest way to the trading post at Shonto, because our horses were dying. That is why we came onto Hopi land."

Esta-qua broke in again. "Who believe *tuva-suh?*"

Longarm decided to take a hand. In a voice as loud as that of the medicine man, but not so harsh, he said, "If you don't believe him, maybe you'll listen to me. We came up here to find out what happened to the three men that some of the Navajos have been whispering around that the Hopis killed."

"You lie like *tuva-suh*, too!" Esta-qua shouted. "We Hopi kill nobody!"

A muttering of agreement began rippling among the elders. Longarm began to wonder if he might not have made a mistake in telling them. He raised his voice above the growing volume of muttering.

"That's why we came up here!" Longarm repeated. "What we came to do is to stop all that talk about the Hopis having something to do with those men dying. The truth's the only thing that'll keep that kind of lies from spreading. There's going to be whispers and ugly words until everybody knows what really happened."

"Then why you sneak in night? Why you not come talk to *wu-ya*? Why you not talk *tu-hik-ya?*" Esta-qua demanded.

For the first time, the elders of the council seemed to be in agreement with the medicine man. He watched the members of the council turning to one another, nodding in approval, speaking to their neighbors in low voices. Over the humming that now filled the room, he said in a low voice to Tosih Nez, "That Esta-qua is smarter than I figured him to be. He's getting them on his side, now. You got any ideas about what to say next?"

Tosih Nez shook his head. "The less I say, Longarm, the better it will be for us. They will believe you, but not me. If there was some way to break their faith in the *tu-hik-ya*—"

"Show 'em he ain't as big a man as he thinks he is?"

"Something like that," Tosih Nez agreed.

"Short of shooting him, I don't know any way we could shut him up. I never have shot a man who wasn't trying to shoot me, but I'd sure be mighty tempted to right now, if they hadn't taken away my guns."

Now the murmuring that had filled the room was beginning to die away. Mumu-ri-wu said, "Esta-qua has asked you a question, Long. We wait to hear your answer."

"You heard about all I got to say, Mumu-ri-wu," Longarm told the Hopi. "What I said is true. I didn't come here to put the blame for the three men dying on your Hopis. I came to find out the truth."

"How *kachada* can do this?" Esta-qua asked loudly. "We know only *alo* have truth! We know *tu-hik-ya* get truth from *alo!* We know *kachada* have no *alo!*" The medicine man dropped into his own language and began speaking to the elders, ignoring Longarm.

His voice pitched so low that only Longarm could hear him, Tosih Nez said, "I think we are losing, Longarm. Esta-qua is bragging about how good a *tu-hik-ya* he is. You would have to pull thunder out of the sky to match what Esta-qua is telling them. Too bad your people don't have any medicine that can do that."

Tosih Nez's words had given Longarm an idea. He thought for a moment and said, "I wouldn't be so sure we don't, Tosih Nez. Maybe I can't beat Esta-qua, but I got a hunch I can wake these Hopis up a little bit."

"How?"

"You'll have to wait and see. Now be quiet a minute. I've got to figure out what I'm going to do before he finishes talking."

Esta-qua was still haranguing the elders. Unobtrusively, Longarm felt in his left hip pocket for the spare bandanna he carried there. The oversized handkerchief was still folded and unused. He thought through the moves he would need to make, not quite sure he could handle the task. He still wasn't sure after he had finished planning, but decided that he had very little to lose. He waited for Esta-qua to stop for breath and then broke into the medicine man's oration.

"Esta-qua!" Longarm called sharply. "You just said Tosih Nez lied to your council. Now I'm saying *you're* lying to them!"

"What I say is true!" Esta-qua protested when he recovered from his surprise.

"You lied when you said the white people ain't got medicine. How come it was us who whipped the Navajos, when you Hopis never could?"

"You had *eamunkin!* They had none!"

"We had guns, Esta-qua," Tosih Nez said. "But they had big *alo*, bigger than our *Un Yei*. It is bigger than your *alo*, too. Else why do the Hopi share lands with us, lands from the whites?"

In the silence that followed Tosih Nez's unpleasant reminder, Longarm put into action the moves he'd been rehearsing in his mind. With his left hand he whipped the folded bandanna from his hip pocket and raised it in a wide arc above his head, flicking the folds free so that the big handkerchief fluttered as it rose.

While the Hopis were following the rise of the bright red-and-white printed cloth, Longarm slid his derringer from his vest pocket. The stubby gun was small enough to be concealed in the palm of his hand, and he kept it hidden while with his thumb he triggered both barrels so quickly that the shots sounded like one. The council chamber echoed with the blast and the heavy conical slugs tore into the floor in front of Esta-qua's feet.

Chapter 10

Before the Hopis could take their eyes from the moving bandanna, Longarm had restored the derringer to his pocket and was holding his right hand in front of him, obviously empty. He let the bandanna flutter to the floor. The Hopis' eyes followed it as it fell. The room was suddenly alive with excited conversation as the elders turned to one another and began discussing the display of white medicine power.

Esta-qua's angry shout overrode the babble. "A trick! It was *eamunkin!*"

"Now, where would I get a gun from?" Longarm reminded him. "You and your snake gatherers took my guns, and Tosih Nez's too, when you jumped us last night."

"This is a true thing Marshal Long says," Mumu-ri-wu said. He looked at Esta-qua. "You put the guns in a safe place?"

"Stah-ne-ta is guarding them," Esta-qua replied sullenly.

"And there's been somebody keeping an eye on us, too," Longarm reminded them.

"It was gun shooting!" Esta-qua insisted. He pointed to the holes in the floor where he'd been standing. "Look!"

"Sure." Longarm nodded. "If you were to dig in the holes you'd find lead, just like bullets." Then, telling the exact truth and hoping none of the elders would ask him to elaborate, he went on, "Except if you looked at those pieces of lead real close you'd see they didn't come out of a sixgun."

"Where, then?" the medicine man asked.

"Now, that's a downright silly question, Esta-qua," Longarm replied. "If I was to ask you to tell me about your medicine, I don't expect you'd tell me much."

Esta-qua scowled as he looked at the two holes in the floor, but so far Longarm had beaten him at every turn. The Hopi looked at the elders, who were gazing at him with displeasure.

Longarm decided it was time to play his hole card, though to do so put him in more risk of having his trick discovered than he liked to take. Still avoiding a direct lie, he swept his hands down the front of his vest.

"Where would I carry a gun in pockets as little as these?" he asked the elders. "And you watched my hands every minute." He nudged the bandanna with the toe of his boot and dragged the limp fabric a few inches across the floor before picking it up and flicking it in mid-air. "You can see there sure ain't no gun in here, either."

"Why have your people never spoken of the white man's *alo* to us before?" Mumu-ri-wu asked.

"Why don't the Hopis and the Navajos tell everybody all you know about the power your gods give you?" Longarm countered.

Longarm was aware that he was treading on very insecure ground. From remembered conversations with Tosih Nez, and from what Esta-qua had said a few minutes earlier, he'd gathered that the Navajo *Yei* meant their gods or the spirits to whom they attributed supernatural powers, and that the Hopi *alo* meant the same thing. He hurried to change the trend of the conversation before any of the elders asked him a question he could not answer.

He faced Esta-qua. "You sure didn't do your people a favor when you hauled us away from the job we were sent to do," he said, watching the faces of the elders over the medicine man's shoulders. "There's three men dead, and a lot of talk's been going around that the Hopis are to blame because you know how to handle rattlesnakes better'n anybody else. Now, two of the dead men were Navajos, and that could start up the old fuss between you and them. There ain't but one thing that'll settle all the talk, and that's finding out the truth, which is what me and Tosih Nez came here to look for. And you're to blame for keeping us from doing it."

Esta-qua started to reply, but Mumu-ri-wu stopped him with a gesture. He said to Longarm, "The council must talk of this. You and the Navajo cannot be in the room while we talk. Will you wait outside the door?"

"Sure. We ain't blaming you for what Esta-qua done. He hurt you more'n he did us by going off half-cocked."

After the uncomfortable warmth of the council chamber, the night air was cool and fresh on their faces as Longarm and Tosih Nez walked out onto the roof of the building.

"I did not know that you *hatinis* had medicine as powerful as that you brought down in there," Tosih Nez said.

"Hell, that wasn't medicine, Tosih Nez. I just played a trick on them Hopis, something I picked up from watching card sharps operate in saloons. I've seen it done time after time."

"I do not understand." Tosih Nez frowned.

"Why, when a card sharp wants to stack a deck, he'll light up a cigar. Everybody looks at the match when he strikes it and follows it with their eyes while he lights up, and all the time the sharper's busy stacking the deck on the table with the hand that nobody's watching."

"And the bandanna was your match and cigar?"

"Now you've got it! But I wish you hadn't reminded me about cigars. I'd sure give a lot to get my hands on my gear right now."

"Do you think that they will let us go?"

"I'd make a money bet they will. They damn sure ain't going to pay attention to Esta-qua."

The Hopi council deliberated for less than half an hour. This time, instead of Longarm and Tosih Nez being ushered into the council chamber by a guard, they were invited in politely by one of the Hopi elders.

"We have judged that Esta-qua is wrong, Marshal Long," Mumu-ri-wu said. "We want as much as the Navajos do to know the truth about the dead men. Please go and find out."

"That's what I was sent to do, Mumu-ri-wu. Just give us back our guns and gear and we'll be on our way as soon as it's light in the morning. But we'll have to borrow horses from you folks to get us to Shonto. I guess that won't put you to much trouble, will it?"

Mumu-ri-wu shook his head. "No. But before you go, there is a thing we would say to the Navajo policeman." He turned to Tosih Nez. "The horses in Wepo Wash worry our people. They want you Navajos to take them away."

"What horses?" Tosih Nez asked.

"Those in Wepo Wash," Mumu-ri-wu repeated patiently. "We do not want Navajo horses grazing on the land the treaty between us has reserved for our sheep herds."

"Navajos do not break treaties." Tosih Nez's voice was sharp. "We have not disturbed the land your sheep graze on."

"Not yet," Mumu-ri-wu replied. "But we have talked in our council of what we will do if you try to take it back from us. We know we are not many, like you *tuva-suh,* and we know you have defeated us in battle many times. But, few as we are, we have agreed we will fight again if we must to keep our range."

"Now hold on," Longarm said. "You know what would happen if the Hopis and Navajos began fighting again. There'd be soldiers in here before you knew it."

"We do not want to fight the Navajos," Mumu-ri-wu told Longarm. "But if we lose the range on which our sheep graze—"

Tosih Nez interrupted. "Wait, Mumu-ri-wu. This thing you talk of, I do not understand. There are no Navajo horses in Kaibito Canyon. You know that our horse herds graze on the range around Chinle Wash, far to the east."

"There is a big horse herd in arroyo of Wepo Wash," Mumu-ri-wu insisted. "What is it, if not Navajo?"

"Ain't the horses branded?" Longarm asked.

Mumu-ri-wu shook his head. "No."

"Are the herdsmen Navajo?" Tosih Nez asked.

"This I do not know. If there are men watching the horses, I do not know of any of our people who have seen them. We only know the horses are there," the Hopi replied.

"Might be just somebody trailing a wild herd to market," Longarm suggested.

Mumu-ri-wu shook his head. "No. If the herd was being

taken to market, it would have gone on. The horses have been there for many days."

"Much of Wepo Wash is in Navajo land," Tosih Nez said. "How is it your people have seen them?"

"We must travel across Navajo land even to go as far as Don Lorenzo Hubbell's trading post. Or to the traders at Shonto, or at Keet Seel. This right we have in the treaty."

"I know," Tosih Nez replied impatiently. "I asked if your people have seen these horses."

"Some have," Mumu-ri-wu replied. He added quickly, "Some who were travelling that way."

"This thing has not been told to the Navajo Police," Tosih Nez said. "I ask you why."

Mumu-ri-wu shrugged. "The horses feed now on Navajo grass, and that is not a thing of our concern. We only want to be sure they do not come on Hopi range. That would make great trouble, even fighting, between us."

"I will go to Wepo Wash," Tosih Nez promised. "I must find out about this thing."

"I'll go along, if you can put it off till we finish the job we came here to do," Longarm said.

"Yes. The horses can wait for a few days. They may even be gone by the time we have finished what brought us here." The Navajo nodded.

"Well, we'll be back at work tomorrow, it looks like," Longarm said. "Now we got the mess Esta-qua stirred up cleared away."

"There is a thing more I have not said," Mumu-ri-wu told Longarm. "You are *quo-cha-da*." He indicated Tosih Nez with a jerk of his head. "He is *tuva-suh*. You have no Hopi with you."

"There is no Hopi police force," Tosih Nez said quickly.

"This is a true thing," Mumu-ri-wu agreed. "But does this make the Hopis less than the Navajos? The killings are of concern equally to our people."

Longarm nodded slowly. "You got a point there, Mumu-ri-wu."

"If you have with you a Hopi, there will be no more asking of questions," Mumu-ri-wu said.

Turning to Tosih Nez, Longarm said, "I don't reckon

it'd bother you?" When the Navajo policeman shook his head, Longarm asked Mumu-ri-wu, "You got somebody in mind?"

"My grandson. He is called Pen-tawi. He is of an age with the policeman, and speaks your tongue. Let him be the eyes of the Hopi."

"That's good enough for me." Longarm nodded. "We'll be leaving at daylight. Tell him to get his gear together and be ready to go along. Which puts me in mind of something. Your man Esta-qua took all our stuff. If we get it back tonight, we won't waste time getting it in shape tomorrow morning."

"Your belongings will be returned at once," Mumu-ri-wu promised. "Your horses will be ready. When you get your own horses at Shonto, leave ours with the trader. Pen-tawi will bring them back to us when he returns."

Longarm and Tosih Nez spent little time in getting their saddle gear ready before spreading their blankets on the floor of the room where they'd been held prisoner.

Puffing a cheroot, Longarm stretched out on his bedroll. He said, "I guess when you're bone tired, even a bed on the floor feels pretty good."

"We *Dineh* say that a bed on stones is better than no bed at all," Tosih Nez replied. "But this day began too early and has gone on too long."

"You think Esta-qua's going to give us any more trouble?"

"No. He will have trouble himself as a result of his stupid interference."

"Then maybe we can go on about our business from now on without anything else taking our minds off it."

Longarm's tenuous bubble of hope did not survive until sunrise. In the gray light of false dawn, while he and Tosih Nez were rolling their blankets ready to carry their gear to the corral, a young Hopi burst into the room.

"Grandfather asks you to come at once to the horse corral, Marshal Long," he said. "There is something of importance."

"You'd be Pen-tawi?" Longarm asked.

"Yes. You will come now, please? I will show you the way."

"Just as soon as we get these bedrolls strapped up."

At the corral, Mumu-ri-wu and two of the other elders were waiting with a third Hopi man.

"Do-yu-ma has brought us serious news, Marshal Long," Mumu-ri-wu said, indicating the stranger. "Another man has died of snake poisoning."

"Whereabouts?"

"Do-yu-ma is not sure exactly where. He knows it was to the north and west, between the Shonto trading post and Black Mesa, but he cannot say where."

"How did he find out about it?"

"He was at the trading post when the Navajo called Hosteen Clau brought news of the dead man there. That was last night."

"Did he know the dead man's name?" Tosih Nez asked.

Mumu-ri-wu shook his head. "No one at the post knew him."

"That is a strange thing." Tosih Nez frowned. "If he was one who traded regularly at Shonto, Hosteen Clau should have known his name and where he was from."

"It ain't going to do any good for us to fret over the whys and wherefores right now," Longarm pointed out. "Not till I get a look at that body. We'll saddle up."

"Our women have cooked food for you to eat before you go," Mumu-ri-wu said. "Will you not eat with us?"

"Now, that's a nice thing for them to do, Mumu-ri-wu," Longarm told him. "And we'd be proud to eat with you Hopi folks any time. If you got something we can chew on while we're riding along, we'd be mighty pleased to have it—"

"There is *pika* and *somoviki*. They can be eaten in the saddle," the elder said.

"That's what we'll do," Longarm said. "We've got a long ride, and I know that Navajos bury their dead by sundown. I want to take a look at that man's body before it's buried."

Chapter 11

Although the Indian Bureau map which Tom Armbruster had given Longarm showed the distance from Tonalea to the Shonto trading post to be only thirty miles, skirting the rough terrain that extended west from the base of Black Mesa added a dozen miles to the distance. Through the long day Longarm, Tosih Nez, and Pen-tawi rode steadily, stopping only to rest the horses in midmorning and midafternoon. They made no stops to eat, but munched *pika* bread or took a *somoviki* from their saddlebags and with their fingers dug chunks of the corn-and-cornmeal stuffing out of the husks in which the bland mixture had been cooked.

There was little conversation. Longarm had been thinking of the problems that lay ahead, and Tosih Nez came from a people which put little stock in idle chatter. Pen-tawi was generally silent. Longarm could not decide whether his grandfather had cautioned him to say as little as possible, or whether the young man was inhibited by having to ride in company with a Navajo, a representative of the Hopis' traditional tribal enemies.

Pen-tawi seemed to be a few years younger than Tosih Nez. His face was full, his lips thick, his nose arched a trifle. His eyes had the overly large pupils Longarm had noticed in others of the tribe, and were dark, with unusually small whites. Pen-tawi wore his hair short, even shorter than Tosih Nez, cut square just above the earlobes and held by a wide headband. He wore no hat and no jacket over his pullover shirt, which was belted at the waist with a narrow leather belt.

In spite of their crescent-shaped detour around the roughest land that extended from the base of Black Mesa, the country they traversed still threw obstacles in their way. Pen-tawi knew the shortcuts, and they moved faster than would have been possible without him.

Always the rugged, ragged bulk of Black Mesa loomed on their right, all but the most prominent features of its upthrust face hidden by the shimmering haze which began to blur the air.

Over country such as they were crossing, swift travel was almost impossible. Longarm set the fastest pace that he could while conserving the strength of their horses, but they had not yet reached their destination when the sky turned to a deep blue overhead and the last thin streaks of daylight were fading above the rim of the distant Kaibab Plateau.

During most of the trip they had ridden abreast, except in places where the trail led them along a narrow ledge or through a steep-walled canyon. They had been able to stay in their wide formation since the sun first disappeared, for they were crossing a wide and relatively level plateau.

Until the dusk had darkened into night they'd been able to see the trail stretching straight ahead of them through the sparse grass, and Longarm had speeded their pace as much as he judged the tiring horses could stand. Ahead of them on the horizon, so far and feeble that it might have been a star, a pinpoint of light appeared. Pen-tawi pointed.

"We are very close now," he said. "That is Shonto."

Though they continued to ride steadily through the night, the light did not seem to grow larger or closer until suddenly through some strange optical illusion created by the thin air of the high desert the light split into two rectangles and the windows of the trading post seemed near enough to touch. A few minutes later they stopped in front of the low, flat-roofed frame building and dismounted, looping the reins of their horses around the hitch rail. Peering through the windows of the trading post, Longarm could see no movement inside.

Walking a few paces away from the patch of light shed through the windows, he lighted a cheroot while he gazed around. Through the sable darkness he could see only one other structure, a building larger than that which housed the trading post itself, a black unlighted hulk fifty yards or so behind the post, which he took to be a barn or storage building. When he scanned the horizon, he saw no other light, no sign that there was another house within a dozen miles.

Longarm shook his head as he peered around. He remembered that Mae Blaisdell had said the trading post was in a deserted area, but he had thought there'd be at least a house or two somewhere close by. He heard a step behind him and looked around to see Tosih Nez approaching.

"I thought there would be something like a town here," Longarm said. "Houses, maybe a place for us to stay tonight."

"We won't sleep on the ground, or on a board floor," Tosih Nez assured him. "And there are houses, *hogans* and *betatkin,* what your people call dugouts, in the shelter of the little valleys. You will see them tomorrow."

"I sure don't see no lights."

"You forget our *hogans* have no windows, Longarm. You are not used to the customs of our people yet."

"I guess not. Well, let's go on in and see what Mrs. Blaisdell's got to say."

Inside the building, blinking in the light of the lantern that hung by its bail from the low ceiling, Longarm looked around curiously. There was no one in the long, narrow room that extended the width of the building. Most of its floor space was taken up by a wide counter which spanned the room. He'd expected the place to be larger than it was. After the description of her stock Mae had given him, he'd also expected to see more merchandise than was displayed in the narrow room.

Blankets, saddle gear, and harness hung on the front wall, some lanterns and a few large pots and pans on the side walls. The wall behind the counter was broken by a door in its center. On each side of the door, extending to the end of the wall, there were shelves on which stood stacks of thick crockery plates and cups, bolts of cloth and ribbon, and large wooden boxes.

Light footsteps sounded and a young woman appeared in the doorway. Her eyebrows lifted in surprise when she saw the three men. Then she smiled at Tosih Nez and said, *"Yehteh-hay, hatalih."*

"Yehteh-hay, shema," Tosih Nez replied.

"Pen-tawi," the girl went on, nodding at the Hopi youth. *"Ha-gohs ha?"*

"Dahtse?" Pen-tawi replied.

Before Pen-tawi could continue, Tosih Nez broke in and spoke a few more quick words in Navajo, then switched to English. "This is Marshal Long. He is from the outside. He is a Federal policeman."

"I am Desiba," she said, speaking now to Longarm. "I work for Mrs. Blaisdell. She has told me of you, and said that you might visit here."

Her voice was very light, and Longarm saw that she was much younger than he'd taken her to be at first glance. Desiba's face was an almost perfect oval. Her nose was slightly uptilted at its wide nostrils. Her mouth was narrow, budded, and very dark red. Below thin brows, her eyes were a lustrous black. Her coal-black hair was parted in the center of her head and brought down below her ears, where it was caught up into twin braids that hung in front of her shoulders almost down to her waist. She wore the universal garb of all the Navajo women he'd seen.

"I'm right pleased to meet you, Desiba," Longarm said. "And I'll be glad to see Mae again."

Desiba shook her head. "She is not here. She has gone to the Mormon colony by the river to attend to some affairs of which she told me nothing. But she will be back soon, I am sure."

Desiba's English had the same precise quality Longarm had noticed in Tosih Nez's speech. She must have had the same schooling. He asked her, "Where around here do the Mormons have a settlement?"

Tosih Nez replied, "They are Mormon missionaries, Longarm. They have built a small town on the big river to the north, a long day's ride."

Nodding, Longarm said to Desiba, "I reckon Mrs. Blaisdell's hired man stayed here to help you run things? Hosteen Clau?"

"He is at his *hogan*," she said. "He has just come back from burying a man who was found dead beside the Marsh Pass trail yesterday."

"That'd be the one who was killed by a rattlesnake?"

Desiba's eyes widened in surprise. She looked questioningly from Longarm to Tosih Nez. "How did you learn of this?" she asked. "It was only yesterday."

"We were at Tonalea," Tosih Nez interrupted. "Answer the Marshal's questions, Desiba. He has come here to find out about these dead men."

Longarm asked her, "That was the man who got snakebit, wasn't it? The one Hosteen Clau was burying?" When Desiba nodded, the lawman went on, "How come they put him in the ground so fast?"

Tosih Nez explained quickly. "If it is possible, Longarm, our people bury the dead before sunset on the day they die."

"Seems like I remember hearing that." Longarm nodded. Then he frowned thoughtfully and asked the Navajo, "Have your people got a law or some kind of holy rule that says that after a body's been buried it can't be dug up again?"

"It is not a custom to do this thing," the Navajo policeman replied with a thoughtful frown. "To disturb a body buried is to disturb the *chindee*. But I can see that it must be done."

"We'll do it first thing in the morning, then," Longarm said. "Hosteen Clau can show us where the grave is. No need to bother him now." He asked Desiba, "Is there a place around here where we can sleep tonight?"

"Travellers who stop here for a night are always made welcome to sleep in the wool barn. There is much room, and the wool bundles make a soft bed. It is the best we have to offer."

"It is a good place, Longarm," Tosih Nez said quickly. "I have slept there."

"That sounds fine to me," Longarm nodded. "I guess we might as well turn in, then."

* * *

"It was there I found him." Hosteen Clau pointed to a rock outcrop at the edge of a juniper bush about fifty yards from the trail. As Longarm pulled his horse off the trail and led them to the juniper, Hosteen Clau continued, "I saw at once that he was not asleep, for if he had lay down to rest he would not have been where the sun could shine on him."

"What about his horse?" Longarm asked. He dismounted and began circling the juniper, examining the ground carefully. "Any sign of it?"

"No." The Navajo shook his head. "And the ground is too hard around the bush to hold a track."

Tosih Nez pointed to a sparse heap of fresh dung fifteen feet or so from the juniper. "Did your horse drop that, Hosteen Clau?" When Hosteen Clau shook his head, Tosih Nez asked, "Did you look around for hoofprints anywhere but by the bush?"

"I did not want to take time to try to find his horse," Hosteen Clau explained. "After I saw the mark of the bite, I knew I must send word of what happened to the *beli-cannas*."

"So you just took the body to Shonto?" Longarm asked.

"I could not let it stay here. Besides, I did not know the man. Someone close to the post might have."

"Did they?"

Hosteen Clau shook his head. "He must have been from far to the east, or maybe the south. No one knew him."

"You are sure the man was Navajo?" Pen-tawi asked. "Not Hopi?"

"He was not of your people, Pen-tawi. He was *Dineh*."

Pen-tawi nodded, apparently satisfied.

"And where did you bury him?" Longarm asked.

"There is a place not far from Keet Seel where many of our people are buried. They picked the place because it was where the *Anasazi* buried their dead when they lived in the old pueblo close by. We took him there to bury, where his *chindee* will have much company."

"I guess that's where we'll head next," Longarm told his companions. "I hope it ain't too far."

"We will get to it before the sun goes," Tosih Nez said. "Unless you wish to find the hoofprints of his horse and

97

follow them. He may have carried something—"

"We'll come back and do that," Longarm interrupted. "What I want to do first is to look at that body while it's still fresh. Let's ride to the grave. We'll track the horse later."

There was less than an hour of daylight left when the party reached the ruins of the settlement which the *Anasazi*, the Ancient Ones, had abandoned long before the first Navajo horsemen swept down from the north. The adobe walls of the old buildings were still standing; in that land of little rain, even sun-dried adobe bricks endured. Hosteen Clau led them past the time-eroded adobe walls to the hump of a little hillock where a rectangle of freshly turned earth showed the location of the grave.

When they had dismounted and looked at the grave for a moment, Longarm said, "We only brought two shovels. Hosteen Clau's likely had his share of shovel work. Tosih Nez, how about you and me doing the digging?"

Tosih Nez took one of the shovels that Hosteen Clau had been carrying tied behind his saddle pad, and Longarm reached for the other. Pen-tawi's hand got to the handle first.

"I have done little work since we started out, Marshal Long," the Hopi said. "Tosih Nez and I are the youngest. Let us do the digging."

Removing the broken earth from the grave was not a hard job, and Hosteen Clau had not dug a very deep hole. Longarm stood close to the grave while the earth was being shovelled out, and when he saw cloth showing when Pen-tawi had lifted a fresh shovelful of dirt, he stopped them.

"Don't dig in deep no more," he advised them. "Just scrape off what's left covering him. If he's got any marks on him besides that bite Hosteen Clau found, I want to look at them and not have to worry about whether they were made before or after he died."

A few minutes more and the body was lifted out of the grave. Ignoring the smell, Longarm began to uncover the corpse. Under the canvas cloth with which Hosteen Clau had improvised a shroud they could already see that the body's right side was swollen.

Uncovered, the swelling was revealed to be so great as to be grotesque. From ankle to waist the puffed flesh was straining at the fabric of the duck trousers the corpse wore. When Longarm finally got the canvas cloth off and exposed the hands and face, their dark amber skin already beginning to draw up taut, Tosih Nez gave an exclamation of surprise.

"That's Soshei Toh! He lived close to Naschetti, almost at the eastern boundary of the reservation."

"You're sure, I reckon?" Longarm asked.

"Of course I am."

"Do you know anything about him besides his name?"

Tosih Nez frowned. "No. I remember him because he wanted me to arrest his nearest neighbor for stealing his allotment money. I found out that Soshei Toh had lost the money gambling, but I could not arrest him just for lying to me."

Hosteen Clau had been watching and listening. Now he asked, "Was I wrong to bury him, Tosih Nez? I sent word when I—"

"You did nothing wrong," Tosih Nez replied. "The way he has swelled up, it looks like a rattlesnake bite."

"Was he swelled this much when you found him?" Longarm asked Hosteen Clau.

"Maybe a little more now than then," the Navajo replied.

"I never saw anybody who died from a snakebite," Pen-tawi remarked.

"You Hopi call the snakes your little brothers. They do not bite you," Tosih Nez said. "Or if they do, you have medicine that keeps the venom from killing you."

Pen-tawi ignored the remark and asked Longarm, "Do they always swell this way?"

"I never saw anybody puff up this much," Longarm said, as he took his clasp knife from his pocket. "It just depends on who's been bit, I guess."

"This is the worst I have seen," Tosih Nez agreed. "But I have only seen a few who died from snake venom."

Longarm hunkered down beside the body and levered the blade of the knife out with his iron-hard thumbnail. He slit the duck trousers from ankle to groin. Relieved of the restraining cloth, the leg puffed still more. From the knee

99

to the top of the slit trouser-leg, the hue of the exposed skin faded from an angry purplish-green around the two small puncture marks inside the thigh to a sickly greenish-yellow at the hip and ankle.

"Them's the biggest fang marks I ever saw," Longarm commented. "Pen-tawi, I reckon you've seen bites on the men in the Snake dance. You ever see the like? Or you, Tosih Nez?"

Squatting beside Longarm, the two Indians examined the punctures closely. Pen-tawi shook his head. "I have not seen very many bites from our little brothers, but these are much bigger than usual."

"I never saw a bite like this, either," Tosih Nez agreed.

"Let's see what else we can find out," Longarm suggested.

He sliced into the taut skin, cutting through the punctures. An unpleasant odor came from the cut as he spread it open with the knife blade, and a small trickle of greenish liquid oozed from the cut. The two small holes had penetrated the dead man's flesh to a depth of an inch or more, and the flesh inside the punctures was a sickly yellowish-tan.

After they had studied the punctures for a few moments, Longarm asked Tosih Nez, "How far apart would you say the fangs are on most rattlers?"

Tosih Nez held his thumb and forefinger half an inch apart. "No more than this," he said.

"And how long are the biggest fangs?"

Tosih Nez placed his thumb at the base of his forefinger's first joint. Longarm turned to Pen-tawi.

"You agree?" he asked. The Hopi nodded, and Longarm went on, "Well, I've been wrong about things before, and I might be wrong this time. But just going by these here holes, I'd say if this fellow was snakebit, it'd have to be the biggest rattler that's ever crawled. I figure if a rattlesnake made these holes, it'd have to be twenty feet long and have a body bigger around than my belly is at the button."

Chapter 12

The Navajo policeman and the young Hopi stared for a moment at Longarm, their faces twisted into puzzled scowls.

Pen-tawi spoke first. "A snake cannot get so big," he said seriously. "It could not find enough food. Rattlesnakes are—" At a loss for words, Pen-tawi spread his hands a yard apart. "Only this big."

"I noticed that when I watched—" Longarm stopped just in time to keep from admitting they had seen the sacred Snake Dance. "When I saw your snake catchers pick some up, out where that Esta-qua fellow jumped us."

"Marshal Long was joking," Tosih Nez told Pen-tawi. "I do not believe that a snake such as he talks of lives anywhere."

"Tosih Nez is right, Pen-tawi," Longarm said quickly. "If snakes do grow that big, it ain't around here."

"If it was not a snake, then..." Pen-tawi frowned. "Is it permitted that I look closer at the wounds?"

"Go ahead," Longarm told him. He moved aside to let the young Hopi get closer to the bisected puncture marks.

Pen-tawi bent close to the gash Longarm had cut and pulled its edges apart. After inspecting it, he put his finger into the cut and rubbed it in the yellowish fluid that had collected at its edges. Removing his finger, Pen-tawi sniffed it with his nose almost touching the finger, then touched the smear with the tip of his tongue. His face wrinkling disgustedly, he spat.

"It is venom from a rattlesnake," he said soberly. "But

very strong, even stronger than the venom our *tu-hik-ya* dry in the sun to use in their medicine."

"I sorta figured that out myself," Longarm said. "It'd have to be, to kill quick and make a body swell up so much."

"And the holes where the venom entered were not made by a snake's fangs," Pen-tawi went on. "They are too big, too deep."

"You got sharp eyes, Pen-tawi," Longarm said. "There's something else wrong with the holes, too. They ain't round, the way a snake's fangs are. They're flat."

"There was talk of an arrow tipped with two points," Tosih Nez suggested. "But I do not think an arrow made this wound."

"Neither do I," Longarm said. "More likely a knife that's had the tip split."

While they talked, dusk had been settling. Hosteen Clau told Longarm, "We must hurry and do what else you wish before it is dark."

"I guess we seen all we need to," Longarm nodded. "We'll get this poor devil buried again, then we can find a place in that old pueblo building and settle in for the night."

Tosih Nez and Hosteen Clau spoke at the same instant. "No," they said. The Navajo policeman added, "We must go as far from the *Anasazi's* homes as we can, Longarm. The pueblo and all the ground around it is *achindee.*"

Longarm did not argue. "Let's get going, then," he said.

Working at top speed, they wrapped the dead Navajo in his shroud again and replaced the body in the grave. The light was nearly gone by the time they had finished. Through the deepening darkness, Hosteen Clau led them far enough away from the old pueblo to avoid offending the spirits of the *Anasazi,* to a shallow arroyo where they made a dry camp. They ate parched corn and jerky, washing the food down with water from their canteens.

Longarm lighted a fresh cheroot before they turned in for the night. As he puffed it, he told them, "We ain't got much choice but to go on back to Shonto tomorrow. We need vittles, and me and Tosih Nez have to buy horses.

102

Then we'll go look for whoever killed that fellow."

"But how will you know where to look?" Pen-tawi asked.

Tosih Nez answered Pen-tawi's question. "We backtrack to find where Soshei Toh was attacked. There will be hoofprints of the killer's horse there. We will follow them until we find him, and our job will be done."

"That may take many days," Pen-tawi said.

"It'll likely take a while," Longarm agreed. "You ain't in a hurry to go home, are you?"

Pen-tawi shook his head. "No. Grandfather would be angry if I did not stay with you until you finish. And there is still the matter of the horses in Wepo Wash."

"We'll get to them after we've found the killer," Longarm promised. "Finding whoever killed four men is a lot more important. And getting some sleep tonight looks pretty important to me right now. We'll let things stand where they are and figure out what we got to do tomorrow on the way to Shonto."

"Looks to me like the best thing for us to do is to split up and ride zigzags back and forth until one of us finds sign," Longarm told Tosih Nez and Pen-tawi.

They had reined in at the spot where Hosteen Clau found the body of Soshei Toh. The time spent at Shonto had refreshed all three of them. A hot supper, which Longarm had persuaded Desiba to cook, a night of sound sleep on the soft wool bales, a hot breakfast before starting out that morning, and the job on which they were now starting did not look as formidable as it had two nights earlier. Longarm wasted no time in starting the search. He picked landmarks and sent the two young Indians to ride on either flank. As soon as they had fanned out, they began the search.

They rode in narrow zigzag patterns within each sector. The only thing they could look for was fresh hoofprints, either on the trail or beside it. The ground was so hard that the weight of a man wearing boots did not break the deep crust of baked soil. While the weight of a horse and rider was enough to leave a faint mark and a wagon's iron-tired wheels cut a shallow flat-bottomed groove, the horse pulling the wagon often left no hoofprints. They followed the

103

wagon-wheel ruts as they set out to try to backtrack the dead Navajo.

Like a serpent's path, the wheel ruts wove in and out of each of the areas they were searching. The tracks veered around the natural obstacles presented by the broken country: hills, grades, rock outcrops, the seams of canyons and arroyos. Horses roamed where wagons could not go; they usually cut across the arcs in the path where wagon wheels swung wide to avoid some obstacle. The hoofprints made by a horse with a man on its back were visible to them from time to time, but they had no way to determine the identity of the riders.

Shortly before noon, Pen-tawi found the saddle-pad and rawhide headstall. Longarm and Tosih Nez joined the young Hopi when he signalled his discovery, and the three hunkered down to inspect the pad at close range.

"Navajo leatherwork," Tosih Nez said positively, fingering the braided headstall.

"And it ain't been here long." Longarm drew his fingertip across the sweat-stained leather pad and studied the thin film of dust that had settled on it. "Less than a week, I'd say."

"We left Tonalea five days ago," Pen-tawi said. "Would two such pads be left on the ground in such a short time?"

"Not likely," Longarm said. "Let's sashay around here a little bit, and see what else we run across."

Riding slowly in overlapping circles while they scanned the ground carefully, their search accomplished its purpose sooner than Longarm had expected. Tosih Nez shouted and waved; Longarm and Pen-tawi reined their horses around and rode to where he had stopped. The Navajo had pulled up at the edge of one of the half-dozen arroyos that cut through the broken surface of the area they were searching.

When Longarm and Pen-tawi drew up beside him, Tosih Nez pointed to the bottom of the arroyo. A dead horse lay on the sandy bottom. From the horse's head, several trails of dry crusted blood snaked across the sand.

"Shot," Tosih Nez said tersely.

They slid down the wall of the arroyo and stopped beside the carcass. Tosih Nez examined the horse's head.

104

"It's a Navajo horse," he told them. "Not shod. Nose rubbed where the headstall fits on. No saddle marks. It must have been Soshei Toh's."

Longarm nodded. "I'd say you're right. And it wasn't shot accidentally. One bullet from the front, right in the brain."

"Why, though?" Pen-tawi asked. "A horse has great value. Who would kill one unless it was injured?"

"A horse ain't worth two hoots in hell to somebody who's killed a man and wants to get away fast," Longarm said. "And whoever it was shot the critter had a horse to ride off on, so there'll be hoofprints around here. Let's spread out and find the prints the killer's horse must've made."

It was Longarm who found the first hoofprints soon after they'd begun circling around the arroyo. In a shallow hollow of the ground where whirling winds had deposited a thin layer of soft sandy soil, he saw the prints of a shod horse with a nail protruding from its off front shoe.

Dismounting, Longarm sat back on his heels and studied the print closely. The rim around the depression the shoe had made when it sank into the soft soil was sharp and well defined. He took a match from his pocket, and, as an afterthought, a cheroot as well. After lighting the long slim cigar, he poked gently with the tip of the match at the soil around the rim of the hoofprint. The dry fragile earth of the rim crumbled instantly, though his touch had been feather-light.

That print ain't been here more'n a few days, old son, he told himself. *But there sure ain't been all that many horses passing by here. And there damn sure ain't more'n one that'd leave the trail unless the rider had a good reason. Like getting rid of a horse and saddle that belonged to a man they killed.*

He turned his attention to the pock at the bottom of the hoofprint, made by the head of a protruding horseshoe nail. The dent was well defined. The nail stuck out far enough to leave an impression on even the hardest ground.

Old son, you really lucked out this time, Longarm mused. *That nail's going to lead you right to whoever it was killed that Navajo. And that'll be whoever killed them others, too.*

105

Standing up, Longarm called for Tosih Nez and Pen-tawi to join him. He showed them the hoofprint.

"That nailhead makes a trail we can follow," he told them. "It'll show up even if the dirt's baked or packed solid. I ain't saying it's going to be easy. You'll have to look real sharp to find them little dents, specially where the ground's rough. But it's all the sign we got that we can be sure of, and we're lucky to have it."

Tosih Nez nodded. "We can follow it, Longarm. It is not much, but it is enough."

Buoyed by their sudden luck, they set out. Riding a few yards apart, they kept their eyes fixed on the baked soil. After the first mile or so, they had learned to judge approximately where to look for the next dent, because they now knew the gait length of the horse wearing the shoe. They also had less difficulty in distinguishing the dent made by the nailhead from other pocks that showed in the dry, unyielding soil, places where a horse or prowling coyote or antelope had disturbed the earth by kicking a small stone loose.

Even when the tracks they were following merged with the regular trail, they could spot the little dents often enough to be sure they hadn't lost it. Such painstaking tracking slowed their progress, for time after time they had to stop and circle a wide area, and often had to dismount and retrace ground they'd passed over, doubling back to the last sure sign they'd seen, before they could pick up the nailhead dents again.

Their job became easier after they'd followed the trail less than two miles, for the tracks left the beaten trail. Now it led them north, once more over soil undisturbed by other hoofprints. They made good progress for half a dozen miles. Then they lost the trail on a rock outcrop and had to circle widely to pick it up again.

Tosih Nez and Pen-tawi shouted only seconds apart, each of them announcing they had discovered the tracks again. Looking from one to the other, Longarm shook his head.

"One of you has got to be wrong," he said. He had been scouting between them, on the outside perimeter of the big arc they'd been covering. Tosih Nez was far to his right,

Pen-tawi to his left. Longarm went on, "When we lost the tracks, we were coming from that way." He pointed to the south. "There ain't a way in the world one horse could go two directions at once."

"I know I am right, Longarm!" Tosih Nez insisted.

"My eyes are as good as yours, *tuva-suh!*" Pen-tawi said hotly. "And I know what I have found."

"Now, just hold on!" Longarm told them sternly. "Both of you put down a rock or something to mark where you picked up them dents, and let's all three of us study this thing out."

They looked first at the tracks Pen-tawi had found. The dents were clearly incised in the hard, bare earth, and Tosih Nez as well as Longarm admitted that Pen-tawi had not been wrong.

Longarm said, "We'll look at yours now, Tosih Nez."

They walked east to where the Navajo had marked the dents he had seen and examined them as closely as they'd looked at those found by Pen-tawi. Again, all three agreed, Tosih Nez had made no mistake in identifying them.

Longarm studied the ground for a few moments and grunted in disgust. "Hell! I ought to've figured it before! Go back to where you found the first sign, Tosih Nez. Pen-tawi, you go to the one you found, and both of you stand straddling the dent."

Their faces showing their puzzlement, the two obeyed him. Longarm stood midway between them and called, "Now, figure out why you two are on different sides of the trail."

For a moment both Tosih Nez and Pen-tawi were silent. Then the Navajo called, "Yes! Since the tracks are on different sides of the trail, the horse passed twice, in opposite directions!"

"But why do the tracks stop and start here?" Pen-tawi asked, his young face showing his perplexity. Then his eyes widened and he said, "He left one of the tracks going, the other coming back. Why are they not connected?"

"Because the trail forks here," Longarm said. "He came from the east, rode south, then came back north and turned west. But why'd he go south at all? What's down that way?"

Tosih Nez said, "A man riding south can only follow the foot of Black Mesa. There are no trails up its face." He thought for a moment and added, "There are a few canyons. And to the south is Denebitto Wash. To reach the top of the mesa is easy for a rider who goes up Denebitto. Most of the canyons become too narrow for a horse to pass through as they slant up to the mesa's top."

"Denebitto Wash?" Longarm frowned. "How much of a ride is that? If it's right close, we might swing down that way and take a look at that horse herd."

Tosih Nez shook his head. "It is too far. We would not get to it before dark."

"We better pass it up, then, and look at the horses later."

Longarm gazed at Black Mesa, only three or four miles distant now. At this close range the heat-haze did not obscure details of its high, rugged face. The westering sun glared on the towering steep flanks of the massive formation, and a glance was all anyone needed to know how it had gotten name. Except for an occasional streak of red or tan sandstone, the face was an island of unrelieved ebony rising like a miniature range of flat-topped mountains from a predominantly reddish terrain.

Shading his eyes with the wide brim of his hat, Longarm glanced at the sun's position. "There's enough daylight left to do some more looking," he said. "If we split up, maybe enough time to find out most of what we need to know. You two men feel like following that trail west while I take the east one?"

"If that's what you think is best," Tosih Nez replied.

"Pen-tawi? You agreeable to riding with Tosih Nez?" Longarm asked the Hopi youth.

"Yes. For a *tuva-suh,* he is a good man."

"We'll do it that way, then. I'll follow the tracks east till I run out of daylight, and turn back. If you run across anything that looks like it'd help to ravel this thing out, stop till I catch up with you. If I don't catch up before it gets too dark to track, make camp and try to scrape up enough splinters of wood for a little fire so it'll be easier for me to find you."

After watching Tosih Nez and Pen-tawi leave, Longarm

started to follow the dim tracks west. He lost sight of the dents now and then, but always managed to find the trail again by getting out of the saddle and walking a short distance. Checking his course by the position of the sun, he found that the dents ran in a fairly straight line. He lost them at last on a wide rock ledge that extended for almost a mile. Though he dismounted and led his horse, hunkering down every hundred yards or so to eye the rock at close range, the surface was too hard to have taken an impression.

Well, old son, there ain't a thing you can do but push on ahead and try to pick that trail up on the other side of this rocky place, he told himself. *And it's been a straight trail so far. Maybe your luck'll still hold good on the other side.*

Across the rocks, where the ledge went underground again, the soil was thin, and baked almost as hard as the rock had been. No nail dents were to be seen on its surface. Longarm rode another half-mile, then another, and was on the verge of turning back and trying to pick up the trail on foot when he saw the cleft ahead. He decided to ride as far as the gap before turning back and dismounting.

He received an unexpected reward. The bottom of the gap slanted upward at a steep angle, and was covered with soft soil that winds had eroded from the surface above and deposited. The first thing Longarm saw was not just the dent left by the head of a horseshoe nail, but the impression of the entire shoe, with the characteristic dent the nailhead made. He could see that the hooves of the last horse that went up the gap had left clear prints all the way to the top of the gap.

Longarm mounted and followed the trail. As his head and shoulders emerged above the mesa's top, he got his second surprise. A large conical tent, a British Union Jack fluttering from the top of its pole, rose from the mesa a hundred yards away. Beyond it a rope corral held a dozen horses. In front of the tent a line of Navajos, men and women, stood shoulder to shoulder. Between the heads of two Navajos near the center of the line the muzzle of a double-barrelled shotgun protruded.

Longarm supposed that the gun pointer was white, but

he could not be sure, for all he could see was the oddest-looking piece of headgear he'd ever laid eyes on. It was a domed hat shaped like a mushroom with a down-slanted visor that hid the shotgun holder's face. Longarm held up his hands and kneed his horse to the top of the mesa.

"Stop right there!" a tremulous, high-pitched voice called. "If you come one step closer I'll shoot!"

Chapter 13

Longarm kept his hands up. He called quickly, "Hold your fire! My name's Long, and I'm a Deputy United States Marshal. All I want to do is talk to whoever this camp belongs to."

"How do I know you are who you say you are?"

There was a clipped crispness to the high-pitched, nasal voice. Longarm had heard enough English voices to recognize the nationality of the speaker. It had been ten years since the British nobility had become fascinated with the idea of owning cattle ranches in the American West and had turned Denver and nearby Colorado Springs into virtual outposts of London.

He called, "If you'll let me get close enough and take down my hands, I'll show you my badge. Will that satisfy you?"

"Very well. You may approach."

His eyes on the shotgun, Longarm toed the horse and it moved forward. Belatedly, he remembered Armbruster mentioning a British professor exploring some of the ancient Indian pueblos on Black Mesa. He was certain he had stumbled onto the professor's camp. Cudgeling his memory, he dredged up the professor's name: R. M. Cranborn.

"I'm going to rein in and show you my badge," he said. "Just don't get nervous with that scattergun."

When he got no reply, Longarm dropped his left hand and reined in his horse. Then he pulled his vest open to show the badge pinned on its lining. The muzzle of the

111

shotgun wavered and was slowly lowered.

A woman pushed through the line of Navajos. Longarm glanced at her and got a fleeting impression that she was tall and looked even taller because of the knee-high laced boots she wore below the tucked-in folds of her split-skirt riding habit. Her face was shaded by the visor of the tan mushroom-domed hat she wore. Longarm did not look at her too closely. He was more interested in watching the muzzle of her shotgun. She examined Longarm's badge, then lowered the butt of the weapon to the ground.

"I suppose you're who you claim to be," she said. "You may lower your arms, Marshal—Long, did you say your name is?"

"Yes, ma'am. Custis Long. I guess this'd be Professor Cranborn's camp?"

"How did you know that?"

"Why, Mr. Armbruster in the Indian Bureau office down at Winslow told me the professor was up here digging around the Indian ruins for relics. Is Professor Cranborn here?"

"My dear man," the woman said, "I *am* Professor Cranborn."

"Professor R. M. Cranborn?"

"Precisely. The R is for Rebecca and the M is for Mary."

Longarm gaped. "I—I beg pardon, ma'am. I didn't think—"

"Of course not," she said. "Few do. Well, dismount if you care to, Marshal. I was just preparing my afternoon tea when the Navajos warned me that a stranger was approaching. I will not apologize for receiving you at gunpoint. Since there have been times in the past when I've encountered difficulties on some of my digs in primitive areas, I always keep this gun on hand. And in case you're wondering, I know how to use it."

"No need to apologize, ma'am," Longarm said as he swung out of the saddle. "Can't say I blame you. A lady off by herself in wild country like this can't be too careful."

"Oh, I've been in wilder places than this, Marshal Long. India—" she pronounced it "Inja," which left Longarm puzzled for a moment—"and Borneo. Jungles, you know. But come into the tent and we'll sit down to chat while we have tea."

Walking behind the professor into the tent, Longarm was surprised to discover that she was almost as tall as he was. The tent's interior was a surprise, too. Longarm got an instant impression of both clutter and carefully planned order.

A large round table stood off-center beside the tent pole. Against the wall on one side stood a stove, a large wooden cabinet, its doors open to reveal a supply of food tins, jars, and boxes, and a smaller table on which stood a spirit lamp with a teakettle on it. A china teapot, cup, and saucer stood beside it.

On the side opposite the stove there was a wide camp bed with a mosquito net draped over it, suspended from ropes that were guyed to the center pole; a large wardrobe trunk, open to display hangers holding clothing; and a canvas contrivance that Longarm had to study for several moments before he identified it as a folding canvas bathtub. Some chairs stood by the table, and Professor Cranborn indicated one of them.

"Do sit down, Marshal," she invited. She took off the hat Longarm had found so interesting and fluffed her hair with one hand while placing the hat on the wardrobe trunk with the other. As she crossed the tent she said over her shoulder, "I'd just started the tea steeping when my *shikari* told me you were riding up our trail. It should be ready by now."

Longarm could not hold his curiosity in check any longer. He said, "You'll excuse me, Professor Cranborn, but I got to ask you what in tunket kinda hat that is you were wearing."

"My sola topee?" The professor was getting another cup from one of the wooden boxes in the food cabinet. "Why, my dear man, I wouldn't think of going outdoors in such hot country without it. It's far superior to the hot, dusty felt hats you men wear." Picking up the cups, she started for the table. "I must apologize, Marshal. It isn't from lack of

113

hospitality that I failed to ask whether you preferred milk or lemon. I've not been able to get either in this isolated spot."

Longarm said hastily, "Oh, I'll just drink it straight, ma'am. I mostly drink coffee, myself."

"After tasting what you Americans call coffee at the railway stations where my train stopped for meals, I cannot understand your preference for it over tea."

"I guess folks from different countries has just got different tastes, ma'am," Longarm said, sipping his tea politely. The first swallow started a tingling on the roof of his mouth. He took a deep breath and went on, "But I must say you fix a nice, strong drink, ma'am. Almost as good as coffee."

"I assume that is a compliment, Marshal. Thank you."

She set her cup in the saucer and looked across the table at Longarm, giving him the first really good look he'd had of her face. It was a long oval that escaped being horsey because of her square chin. Her nose was thin and aquiline, with high-arched nostrils. Her mouth was large, and her lips just missed being too thick. Her eyes were china blue, and the puff of hair that was held in a roll to disguise a forehead a trifle too high was taffy blonde. She was younger than Longarm had imagined her to be, probably still a few years short of forty, he told himself. The jacket she wore effectively disguised her figure.

If the professor was aware of Longarm's survey she gave no sign of it. She was looking thoughtfully into her teacup while he scanned her face, and he noticed a frown forming on her lips.

She looked up suddenly. "Is your American West really as uncivilized as I've heard it described, Marshal Long?" she asked.

"It ain't exactly what you'd call tame, I guess, but maybe it'd be better to say it just ain't settled down yet." He took a cheroot from his vest pocket, flicked his thumb across the head of a match, and puffed the cigar to light. Professor Cranborn had said nothing, and he saw that she was waiting for him to go on. He said, "Are them Navajos that's working for you making trouble?"

"Not exactly. There are some ruins in the area where I'd planned to dig, and they refuse to go near them. I understand their primitive superstitions, so I'll return later with some white workmen for that. What I'm concerned about are horsemen who've come near the camp several times, always at night. From the glimpses I've managed to get of them, they're white men."

"Have they bothered you? Stolen anything?"

"No. All they've seemed to want to do is look at my camp. I've called to them two or three times, but they've just ridden off without answering."

"They always come at night? Never in the daytime?"

"Always at night." She nodded. "Whatever could their purpose be, Marshal Long?"

"Well, you got me stumped, Professor Cranborn." Longarm paused thoughtfully, then went on, "I'm on a case right now that I can't get away from. It looks like I'll have it wound up in a few days, though. When I do, I'll stop back by and do some noseying around and see what I can find out. That suit you?"

"I'd appreciate it very much, Marshal. I'm not frightened, you understand, but if there are any criminals in the vicinity—"

"Sure. I follow you, Professor."

"Thank you. Now let me pour you another cup of tea."

Longarm stood up. "I better not stay any longer, Professor, but I got to be getting along. I'll run out of daylight to get back to where they'll be waiting. But as soon as my case is closed, I'll find the time to ride this way again and see what I can find out."

"Are you sure you can't stay for another cup?" she asked. "The tea's already brewed, all I have to do is pour it."

"Thank you for the cup I drank, and for the offer, Professor, but I got to be getting along. I'll run out of daylight before I get to where my men are waiting if I stay."

"Drop in any time you're passing, Marshal Long. I promise not to meet you with a shotgun next time."

Longarm had ridden across the mesa almost to the cleft by which he'd ascended when the thought occurred to him. *Old son, finding that professor's a lady got you so snarly*

115

you forgot what you ought to've done. Now, there was a set of tracks showing that loose horseshoe nail leading up the gully, but there wasn't none going down. And you didn't look at them horses in that rope corral.

Wheeling the horse, Longarm rode back to the tent. Professor Cranborn had not yet gone inside. As he pulled up, she asked him, "Did you forget something, Marshal, or did you change your mind about having another cup of tea?"

"I was going to take a look at them horses of yours before I left, and I plumb disremembered to do it. You don't mind if I just glance at 'em, do you?"

"I don't mind in the least, but they're not my horses. They belong to the Navajos."

"Well, I guess it'll be all right with them."

Longarm dismounted and walked over to the rope corral, Professor Cranborn following him. It took him only a few minutes to determine that, like all Navajo horses, these were unshod. He ducked back under the rope and touched his hat brim.

"I thank you again, Professor."

"You didn't find what you were looking for? Or did you?"

"You might say that I did and I didn't. Anyways, I'll be on my way. But, like I told you, I'll come back and do some scouting around soon as I close my case."

"I'll be expecting you to call, then."

Longarm touched his hat brim again and started the horse moving toward the cleft. *That professor lady sure acts like she is what she says she is, old son,* he thought. *But there's something fishy about that set of tracks that came up here and never did go down. It'll take more'n one man to cover this whole mesa looking for tracks. That's a job for you and Tosih Nez and Pen-tawi, all three. And it'll have to be done if that trail the young fellows is on peters out. So you just might be calling on the lady again sooner than she thinks.*

Guided by the landmarks he had noted while riding east, Longarm made fast time running to the spot where he and his companions had parted. The sun hung low and was taking on its pre-sunset color, but there was still ample light for him to follow the trail of nailhead dents and catch up with Tosih Nez and Pen-tawi before dark.

Even though he had not pushed his horse, Longarm reached the pair sooner than he'd expected. Tosih Nez and Pen-tawi had covered only eight or nine miles from their starting point. They were not mounted, but had drawn their horses together and were sitting on the ground in the shade the animals' bodies cast.

"I figured you'd've got further than this," Longarm said when he was close enough to talk without shouting. "What's wrong? Did you lose the trail, or just get too tired to move fast?"

"Not either," Tosih Nez replied. "Bad luck."

He held out a horseshoe nail. Longarm took it and looked at it closely. The nail's head was bent at a slight angle to its flat, tapered length. It was as shiny as burnished silver, far brighter than the color its metal had been when newly forged, mute evidence of the head's having been scoured by countless millions of tiny grains of abrasive sand each time the horse had touched its foot to the ground.

"Bad luck's right. I don't guess any of us figured on that loose nail just dropping out. Did you pick it up right here?"

Tosih Nez shook his head. "Back half a mile. We tried to find tracks after we found the nail, but the ground is too hard."

As he usually did when he couldn't find words to fit the occasion, Longarm lighted a cheroot. He looked at the nail again for a moment and dropped it in the pocket of his vest with his matches. "Well, that stops us following the track going this way. But it ain't all she wrote."

"You found sign where you were?" Tosih Nez asked.

"Enough for us to get a fresh start." He gave them an abbreviated version of what had happened, and concluded, "We'll just go back to the top of Black Mesa and start tracking in the other direction."

"What do you expect to find?" Pen-tawi asked.

"Damned if I know," Longarm replied. "But the other end of the trail is the only place we got to start from now."

"Will we go back tonight?" Tosih Nez asked. He added, "The moon is nearly full. It will be light enough to travel."

Longarm shook his head. "No. It'd be too dark to pick

up a trail. Seeing as we ain't more'n five or six miles from Shonto, we'd better ride on back there and buy enough vittles to keep us going a week. We won't lose any real time. We can start before daylight tomorrow and be at the mesa by noon. If that suits you, we'll move on right now."

Darkness had fallen when they reached their destination and reined in at the trading post, but the bright moon made the landscape almost daylight-bright. As their footsteps grated on the floor, Mae Blaisdell came through the door behind the counter.

"Longarm!" she exclaimed, a smile parting her full red lips. "Hosteen Clau and Desiba told me you'd been here and gone. I was afraid you might not come back."

"You know I wouldn't've left these parts without seeing you, Mae. I sorta counted on seeing you when we was here before."

"I had to go to the Mormon settlement, but I guess Desiba told you that. I just got back yesterday." She started around the counter, stopped, and said, "I hope you didn't eat supper on your way here."

"We didn't," Longarm replied. "We figured it'd be better to put off eating until we got here."

"That's good. Desiba and I were just getting ready to eat, and there's plenty for all of us. I brought back some freshly cut beef steaks, and the two she's cooked are far too big for us, so we can divide them and start eating while she cooks some more."

While Mae was talking, Hosteen Clau came in the front door. He did not interrupt her, but greeted Longarm and the others with a wave and a smile. Hosteen Clau exchanged a few words in Navajo with Tosih Nez, who nodded, his face breaking into a smile.

Hosteen Clau told Mae, "Fixed up horse. No more work to do. Go to *hogan* now, eat supper." He indicated Tosih Nez and Pen-tawi with a gesture and added, "They come to eat with me."

Before Longarm could open his mouth to object, Tosih Nez said quickly, "It's better Pen-tawi and I visit Hosteen Clau, Longarm. You and Mrs. Blaisdell will want to talk."

"You know you're welcome to stay," Mae said, but it

was clear from the look on her face that she liked the idea, too.

"We know," Tosih Nez said. "But I am hungry for Navajo food. And it will do Pen-tawi good to eat with *Dineh*."

"It's all right with me, if that's what you both want to do," Longarm told Tosih Nez. "We can make our plans later on."

Longarm followed Mae into her living quarters. Desiba must have been listening, for she had already put a third plate on the table and was adding a knife and fork when they went in.

"Don't look for Harvey House china and silverware here," Mae smiled. "It's easier to use what we stock in the store."

"I found out a long time ago that crockery don't make grub taste better," Longarm told her. He looked at the plain thick plates, wooden-handled steel knives, and three-pronged forks on the table. "This is just about my style, Mae."

Desiba's presence inhibited conversation between Longarm and Mae during the meal. Longarm finished eating first. He crossed his knife and fork on his cleared plate and put a cheroot in his mouth. He fumbled in his vest pocket for matches and brought out four or five as well as the horseshoe nail. He laid the nail on the table beside his plate while he lighted the cheroot.

"What on earth are you doing with that nail?" Mae asked.

"Oh, it's just a sort of clue. Not that it's much good now."

Longarm gazed at the nail. His eyes strayed to the plate. Something about the crossed knife and fork seemed to bother him, but he could think of no reason, and that bothered him, too. He sat frowning at the utensils until Mae spoke.

"Longarm, let's go for a little walk and get out of Desiba's way while she cleans up."

"Why, sure. It'd be good to stretch my legs."

"Wait outside then, if you don't mind, while I freshen up."

"If we walk down by the corral, we won't have to worry about people watching," Mae suggested as she joined Longarm.

119

They strolled through the brilliant moonlight to the corral, Mae's hands clasped around Longarm's biceps. As they drew near the pole enclosure, she released one hand and began to stroke Longarm's crotch.

"You don't know how much I've hoped you'd come to see me," she said, fumbling with the fly of his trousers and having little success in unbuttoning it.

Longarm brought his left hand down to help her. Mae took her hand away and stretched out her arm. It was not a normal gesture, and Longarm looked up. Just as he raised his head, Mae brought her arm down with a sharp snap. Longarm saw a strange object, like a black wand, appear in her hand. His sixth sense warned him in time and he grabbed Mae's arm as it descended.

She twisted her wrist and Longarm felt a prickle of pain on the back of the hand that was holding her arm. He shook the arm. The black object Mae had been holding dropped to the ground. Longarm looked at it. The bright moonlight showed him a fork such as the one he'd used at dinner. This one was different, though. The middle tine had been removed.

"Godamighty!" Longarm gasped, grabbing Mae's free hand.

He knew now who had killed the three Navajos and the Indian Bureau clerk, and how. What he did not know was why.

Chapter 14

Mae was still struggling, trying to get hold of the fork that Longarm had knocked to the ground. With the toe of his boot, he shoved the weapon out of her reach and got hold of her free arm. Pulling both arms behind her, Longarm encircled her wrists with his right hand, and clamped them together. It took all the strength of his powerful muscles to hold the twisting, writhing woman, but after a few moments Mae realized she could not break his iron grip and stopped fighting.

"Damn you, Longarm!" she gasped. "How did you know?"

"I didn't. I noticed the forks on the table at supper, and they reminded me of something, but I couldn't bring to mind what it was. Then when you took out that one you were carrying in your sleeve, and I saw it, I remembered Hosteen Clau had said he'd had to fix up your horse, and recalled how you got upset when you saw that horseshoe nail we picked up on the trail. And when you tried to stick me with that fork, it all came together."

"I knew I'd made a mistake when I asked you about the horseshoe nail," Mae said, as much to herself as to Longarm. "My horse's shoe came loose halfway back from the Mormon settlement, and I told Hosteen Clau to fix it. But when you pulled the nail out of your pocket, I thought you'd connected it with me in some way. I guess I panicked."

"I guess you did," Longarm agreed.

While he'd listened to Mae, he'd become conscious that

his left hand was beginning to throb. He glanced at it. The moonlight showed an angry welt on its back, and a few drops of coagulating blood. Longarm had been only half aware of the scratch he'd gotten while he struggled with Mae. Now he realized that the concentrated rattlesnake venom smeared on the tines of the fork had gotten into his blood.

"Come on," he said, pulling Mae away from the corral.

She saw where Longarm was taking her. "Why are we going to the barn?"

"I left my coat and some of my gear there, and I aim to get the handcuffs on you before you do any more damage."

Mae started struggling again, but Longarm had no time now to be gentle. He dragged her to the barn as fast as her resistance would let him. Mae had no chance against his greater strength, and Longarm got the cuffs on her, pinioning her hands behind her back. Mae gave up the uneven struggle after the cuffs closed on her wrists, but by this time the rattlesnake venom was beginning to take effect on Longarm.

He looked at his hand and saw it had started to puff up, and he could feel his left arm prickling all the way to his shoulder. He dug what was left of his bottle of Maryland rye out of his saddlebag and took a big swallow, but even Tom Moore could not help him this time. The snakebite symptoms grew steadily worse. Tucking the bottle under his arm, he grabbed Mae's wrists.

"Come on," he told her harshly. "We're going back to your house, where I can get some help. If you know what's good for you, you'll behave, and not make me have to handle you rough."

Mae walked along docilely enough as Longarm led her back to the trading post building, and called Desiba from the living quarters. Desiba's eyes goggled when she saw the handcuffs, but Longarm gave her no time to ask questions.

"Get over to Hosteen Clau's *hogan* fast," he ordered the Navajo girl. "Tell Tosih Nez and Pen-tawi to come running."

Longarm bustled Mae into her living quarters and pushed

her into a chair. He sat down facing her and lighted a cheroot. His hand and arm were swelling rapidly, and he could feel his mind growing cloudy. He fought the symptoms of the spreading venom as he looked at Mae. She glared at him, her eyes slitted with anger, her chin thrust out, her lips compressed.

"You can maybe save yourself from hanging if you talk," Longarm began. "I can put all the pieces together, now I got a start, but it'll take me less time if you tell me what you know."

Mae stared at Longarm unblinking, her jaw firmly set, the thin line of her compressed lips unchanged.

"Damn it, Mae!" Longarm went on. "There's got to be a reason why you killed four men! And seeing that you didn't balk at killing, I got a pretty good hunch I'm going to find you done a lot more than I know about now when I start digging deeper into this case."

Unexpectedly, Mae spoke. "I did what I had to do, Longarm."

"Nobody's got to murder folks," Longarm said.

"Are you trying to make me believe you've never killed anybody?" she asked.

"No. There's a difference between murder and killing, Mae. I've killed men, but only when it's been them or me, or to keep them from killing somebody that didn't deserve to die."

"Do you have any children, Longarm?" she asked suddenly.

Longarm frowned. "What's that got to do with it?"

"Because I have a child. A daughter. She was—well, her father and I didn't get married, for a lot of reasons that don't matter right now. That was nearly twenty years ago. But I had the choice of doing what I was told to do, or have my girl murdered. What would you have done?"

Longarm's mouth was dry. He had to force himself to speak. "Go on, Mae. Who made you do it? And why?"

"Right now, I'd like nothing better than to tell you. But I can't, because I don't really know."

"Somebody gave you orders, if you're telling me the truth."

"Oh, yes. I was—" Mae broke off as the scuffling of running feet sounded outside. She said hurriedly, "I won't tell you anything unless we can talk alone, where no one can hear us."

Longarm could tell from the firmness in her voice that Mae would not change her mind.

Tosih Nez and Pen-tawi ran in, accompanied by Hosteen Clau. Desiba followed them. Longarm struggled to keep alert. The venom had spread throughout his system by now. He was sweating profusely, and waves of nausea were coming and going. He summoned all his resources and found the strength to give Tosih Nez and Pen-tawi a quick summary of what had happened. Hosteen Clau and Desiba listened, too, their faces growing first sober, then fearful as Longarm unfolded his story. When he mentioned that the venom-coated fork had scratched his hand, Pen-tawi interrupted.

"Wait," the Hopi youth said over his shoulder, starting for the door. "I go to get my pouch. Maybe what I have will help."

Longarm was growing dizzier by the minute, but he forced himself to hold on. He told Tosih Nez, "The nearest jail's at Winslow. How long'll it take you to get Mae there and come back?"

"Eight days, if I travel some by night. But what about you?"

"Hell, I'll be all right. I feel a little bit dizzy right now, but I'll get over that after a while."

"If Pen-tawi goes with me, we can cross the Hopi lands," Tosih Nez suggested. "Then we can be back in six days."

"Take him along, then. When you get back, we can wind up this case in pretty quick order, with what I know now."

"Are you sure you will be all right?"

Desiba interrupted them. She spoke for the first time, in Navajo, to Tosih Nez. He answered her and told Longarm, "Desiba promises she will care for you. I think you can trust her."

Before Longarm could answer, Pen-tawi returned. The Hopi youth carried a small parcel wrapped in snakeskin. He opened the bundle and gave Longarm a thin wafer baked from the white Hopi cornmeal.

"Chew this, and swallow only a little at a time," Pentawi said. "And I have ground roots here to make tea. You must drink it very hot, all night."

"Give the roots to Desiba," Tosih Nez said. "You and I, we will start now with the *shema*, to Winslow."

Those were the last words Longarm heard. He had bitten off a piece of the cornmeal wafer and was chewing it. He swallowed the bite and started to give Tosih Nez more instructions, but found his lips had grown numb. He mumbled a few unintelligible sounds and then blackness took him.

Consciousness returned to Longarm almost as swiftly as he had lost it. His first awareness of the world was the light that filtered through his closed eyelids. He did not open his eyes at once. His mind was slow to register the sensations his nerves were sending to his brain. Longarm was first aware that he was ravenously hungry. Then he realized he was lying naked in a bed.

He opened his eyes and looked around a room that was strange to him. Light filtering through a gauzy curtain of the room's single window showed him clothing hanging on wall pegs, but he could see few details. Along one wall stood a small dresser. He started to get up, but the best he could manage was to prop himself on an elbow while he continued to study his surroundings.

His Winchester, still in its saddle scabbard, was standing in one corner, his boots beside it. He looked along the wall again and this time he identified his gunbelt and on the peg next to it, his vest hanging on one of the pegs, the legs of his covert-cloth pants dangling below it. Then memory came back in a sudden flood and he knew where he was and why he was there. He felt his left arm. It was no longer swollen. He looked at the scratch on his hand. It was covered by a narrow brown scab.

Raising his voice, he called, "Anybody around here?"

Across the room a door opened. Desiba came in. She

smiled and said, "Pen-tawi told me true. You wake just when he said you would, Longarm."

"How long was I out?"

"Two nights, one day."

"He tell you I'd be hungry?"

"Yes. I have food ready to prepare. I will bring it to you soon. You are not to get up. Maybe tomorrow. Pen-tawi said."

"Whatever that stuff was he give me, it sure worked."

"It is not for nothing that the Hopi call the rattlesnakes their little brothers," Desiba observed. "They know things we of *Dineh* have not learned."

"I guess I was lucky he was here."

"Yes. He said the poison on the fork was very strong."

"He found the fork where Mae dropped it?"

"She told him where to look."

"I hope he put the damn thing in a safe place. Somebody that didn't know better could get hurt if they picked it up."

"It is here. I have it in a box."

"I'd like to take a look at it," Longarm said.

"Of course." Desiba went to the shelf, brought back a small box, and handed it to Longarm. "You look at it while I fix you food. You must eat much to get strong fast again."

Longarm opened the box and looked at the fork. It was just as he'd remembered from the fleeting glance he'd had in the moonlight: one of the forks Mae kept in her stock, a three-tined steel table fork with a black wooden handle. However, this fork had been altered by breaking the center tine at the shaft and grinding the two that remained to needle points with razor-sharp edges. A coating of light amber gum still clung to the tines.

You were lucky, old son, Longarm told himself grimly. *If Mae'd got the points in you real deep, you'd be pushing up daisies now instead of lying here waiting for your supper, or breakfast, or whatever meal it is Desiba's fixing.*

Longarm felt better after he'd eaten. After a while, the food or the exhaustion brought on by his body's internal struggle to recover made him sleepy and he dozed off. The room was dark when he woke up, but he could see Desiba sitting in a chair by the bed. He called her name.

"I am here, Longarm," she replied.

"Yes, I see you. You been sitting up with me every night?"

"Of course. The first night I had to give you the root tea. Then I had—" She hesitated before saying, "Your body threw out the poison, and I needed to wash it from your skin."

Longarm understood more than the Navajo girl had said. He told her, "Thank you, Desiba. I don't know what else to say."

"Say nothing." She stood up. "You must eat again. I will bring you something."

Longarm woke again, in the early daylight, and ate yet again. He went back to sleep almost at once, and dusk was near the next time he awakened. Even without trying to move, he knew he was rapidly regaining his strength. He sat up, moving easily, and swung around on the bed until his feet rested on the floor. He got to his feet much more easily than he'd thought possible, and was standing beside the bed when Desiba came in.

"You should stay in bed," she protested. "I am here to bring you food and do what else you want."

Longarm was suddenly aware that he was naked, but Desiba was paying no attention to his nudity. It dawned on him then that his body was anything but strange to her, after she'd tended to him while he'd lain helpless in the two-day stupor from which he was just recovering. He decided to follow her example and ignore the fact that he was naked.

"Now, it's all right, Desiba," he said. "I just want to stand up for a minute or two and see how it feels."

"Are you sure you are strong enough?"

"I feel pretty strong right this minute. You've been feeding me good, and I guess all that rattlesnake poison's out of my system by now."

Desiba nodded. "Yes. Pen-tawi said that when you had purged the poison you would be well at once. I—I guess it will not be bad for you, then. But you must go back to bed soon, and I will bring you supper."

"You go ahead and start getting the grub ready. I'll be in bed by the time you get back."

Longarm kept his word and was in bed when Desiba returned with his food. He ate, and when she'd taken away the plate, got up and walked without any real unsteadiness to the corner where his saddlebags lay beside his rifle. He took out a handful of cheroots and the oilskin packet in which he carried his spare matches and returned to bed. He was propped up on the pillows puffing a long, thin cigar when Desiba came back into the room.

"You do feel strong, to go across the room alone and find your cigars," she said. "I am glad, Longarm."

"No gladder than I am. And you got to be tired out after them nights you set up with me. You can get some sleep in your own bed now."

"I have not minded, truly. If you want me to stay—"

"There's not any use to, Desiba. I can look after myself all right. You go to bed whenever you got a mind to."

"You want nothing more now?"

"Not a thing. I'll blow out the lamp when I'm ready to go to sleep, and you don't have to worry about me till breakfast."

Longarm did not stay awake long after Desiba had left him. He finished his cheroot, got up to blow out the lamp, and went back to bed. He fell asleep at once, and was still sleeping soundly when he felt a finger brush across his lips. He opened his eyes and saw Desiba bending over him.

Her voice softly pleading, she whispered, "I am not worried now about you, Longarm. I am thinking about myself. Is it all right if I come to bed with you?"

Chapter 15

"There ain't a thing I'd like better'n for you to come in with me, Desiba," Longarm told her.

Desiba stood erect, letting the white shift she wore slide off her shoulders and down her body to the floor. She stood there for a moment. Longarm could see her body only as a dim outline: a round face with two dark blurs for eyes and a small shadow of a mouth; tawny shoulders; the shading under high, small breasts with dark rosettes at their tips; narrow hips and the line of shadow that divided her thighs, topped with a wispy black pubic brush.

He threw off the light blanket that covered him, and Desiba lay down beside him. She snuggled up to him and her hand brushed over the mat of crisp brown curls that covered his chest.

"I often wondered something when I was washing you while you were sleeping," she said thoughtfully.

"What was that?"

"Why you white-skinned men have fur on your bodies, and men of *Dineh* only smooth skin."

"You got me there. That's something I wouldn't know."

Desiba's hand was moving across Longarm's stomach now, down to his groin. His erection had not started yet. Desiba circled her fingers around his shaft for a moment, then slid her hand along its flaccid length.

"I wondered too, if all of you are so big. So much bigger than *Dineh* men," she whispered.

"I never knew we was. Have you been with many men, Desiba?"

"Not many. Five—almost six."

"Almost six? How's that?"

"One man I wanted to have me could not grow stiff. He was white, like you, not *Dineh*." She felt Longarm swelling under the caresses of her fingers. "But you grow hard quickly. And even bigger than I thought."

Longarm turned on his side and bent to kiss her. Desiba turned her head away.

"Don't you want to kiss?" he asked.

"It is not our way. I do not know how."

"Maybe I can show you."

Longarm pressed his lips to hers. Desiba remained passive for a moment or two, then her lips grew firm under his. Gently, a bit at a time, Longarm parted her lips with the tip of his tongue and after a few seconds she opened her mouth to him and their tongues met. He did not hold the kiss too long.

"Did you like it?" he asked.

"I am not sure. It makes me want you in me more. Is that why you kiss, Longarm?"

"One reason, I guess."

"All I know is that I want you in me now."

Longarm lowered his head. His lips found the soft, pulsing hollow at the base of her neck and he began caressing it with the tip of his tongue. Her woman smell filled his nostrils, a mixture of musk and spices. Desiba shivered and tightened her grip on his swelling shaft. He traced a path from her neck down to her breast, found her rosette pebbled, the nipple protruding stiffly. He took the rosette into his mouth and ran his tongue around the small, hardened nipple.

Desiba's back arched. She threw her thigh over Longarm's hip and began rubbing her scanty pubic brush against his upthrust tip. He pushed forward and went into her shallowly. The muscles of Desiba's small, gently rounded abdomen tightened. She inched closer to him and tugged at Longarm's shaft to pull him into her, but he rolled away. Desiba whimpered and groped at his groin until she found his erection, now throbbingly hard.

130

"Come back into me, Longarm!" she urged. "All the way in! I ache for you inside!"

Longarm moved toward her and Desiba positioned him again. This time he drove in swiftly and buried himself in one quick lunge. Desiba groaned as he neared the end of his thrust and Longarm stopped and held himself motionless.

"You ain't ready yet," he said. "I don't aim to hurt you."

"Hurt me, Longarm! Hurt me hard! This is why a woman wants a man! I knew you would hurt me when I saw your size, while you slept from the poison! I ache for you to hurt me!"

Longarm rolled to bring his body above Desiba. She was even smaller than he'd realized. Her head came only to the base of his throat, and he hesitated before lunging. Desiba was groaning again, and her hips were rearing up urgently. This time he did not let Desiba's groans stop him. He pushed aside his compunctions and finished his stroke, his shaft penetrating her until their hips met with the soft smacking of flesh on flesh.

"*Aie-ee!*" Desiba screamed. "I hurt but I feel good!"

Longarm began stroking. He had driven into her only half a dozen times when Desiba cried out again and her body shivered then quaked as her orgasm gripped her. Longarm slowed his stroking but did not stop. It seemed to him that he'd no sooner carried her through her spasm of fierce shaking and small screams than she began another. After the jerking of her hips had ended and her cries of delight subsided, she looked up at him.

"Are you not finished yet?" she asked.

"No. Not yet. Not for quite a while yet. Not unless you want to stop."

"No, no. I only thought—"

Longarm stopped her words with a kiss, arching his body to bring his lips down to hers. His new position parted her thighs even wider. He sank into her and began stroking slowly. Desiba squirmed, and the breath rasped through her nostrils. Sooner than Longarm had expected, smothered moans trembled in her throat and her hips began thrashing wildly as she responded to his continued deep, firm penetrations. She jerked into her climax and when Longarm felt

131

her growing limp he ended their kiss. He had begun to build to his own climax now, and did not want to race to meet Desiba when her next spasm began.

Desiba recovered more slowly this time. Longarm prolonged their embrace until he felt the rolling of her hips grow faster. Then, as the ecstatic moans that marked the start of her spasms began pouring from her lips, he speeded his thrusts, letting himself build faster.

Desiba's moans rose to a crescendo of wild cries. Longarm had timed well. He was past control now and drove home his final strokes to the accompaniment of Desiba's flooding warmth that matched his own prolonged jetting. Her wails died down. Longarm let himself fall forward while he shook in his own final draining.

Desiba's small body stirred under his after they'd lain without moving for several minutes. Longarm moved aside and they lay apart in silence for a while. Then Desiba sighed, a long, slow sigh of satisfaction.

"Is it always this way when you are with a woman?" she asked Longarm.

"I try to make a woman happy, if that's what you mean."

"You must have made many women happy, Longarm. I think I am going to be unhappy when you must go."

"Let's don't talk about that now. I ain't going anyplace for a while. Except, right this minute, I feel like going back to sleep."

"Do you wish me to leave you?"

"I didn't say that." He slid his arm under Desiba's small body and pulled her closer to him. She sighed contentedly as she rested her head on his shoulder. Longarm stretched luxuriously. His eyes closed slowly as sleep claimed him.

"Are you sure it would not be wiser to wait for Tosih Nez and Pen-tawi to return so they can go with you?" Desiba asked.

She was standing beside Longarm at the corral fence. Inside the corral the crowbait gelding he'd bought to replace his dead horse stood saddled and ready. Four days had passed since his recovery from the rattlesnake venom, and

132

when Tosih Nez and Pen-tawi still had not returned, Long-arm had gotten edgy.

"They ought to've been back by now," Longarm told her. "Something's happened that's holding 'em up. The Hopis are worrying about a herd of horses up at the head of Wepo Wash, and I'm going to save some time scouting things out."

"Are you sure they will be able to find you?"

"From what I saw when we were following Mae back here the other day, Tosih Nez and Pen-tawi are both good enough trackers so they can just about follow me by the butts of these fool cigars I keep saying I'll stop smoking and never do. You just tell 'em I'm going back that same way, and if I leave the trail, I'll put up a rock marker. They know the country. They'll find me, all right. Someplace up Wepo Wash."

"You will be back here, to say what to do about the post?"

"Soon as I can make it. But you and Hosteen Clau can keep things going for a while."

"Yes. We will do our best."

"It'll all work out, Desiba. Just go along the way you have been, and don't worry."

Heading east, covering the same ground that he and his companions had tracked over so laboriously when they were moving in the opposite direction, Longarm moved swiftly. He no longer had to stop and look for hoofprints in the hard soil. The only stops he made were short ones, and he halted only long enough to keep his horse from tiring. The key landmarks along the route were fresh in his memory, and he pushed on through the day's increasing heat toward the biggest landmark of all, Black Mesa.

Soon after noon the mesa's serrated rim appeared through the shimmering heat-haze that was now dancing above the baked earth. The mesa's bulk seemed to grow and the height of its ebony face to increase as he drew closer. Riding steadily, early in the afternoon Longarm was so near the mesa that it no longer served him as a landmark. For guidance he now referred more and more to features of the terrain: an isolated formation of red sandstone, the thin slit of an arroyo's tail cutting a zigzag slice into the surface of the barren soil, the gnarled skeleton of a water-starved juniper.

He reached the spot where he and Tosih Nez and Pentawi had turned west toward Shonto following Mae's trail from Black Mesa's face, and reined in. Dismounting, he found three flat rocks and stacked them one atop the other. Then he placed a single pebble on the south side of the miniature cairn to indicate the new direction in which he'd be riding. Lighting a cheroot, he looked at the cairn for a moment, remembering his promise to Professor Cranborn to return soon and investigate the night riders who'd been visiting her camp.

You know, old son, it ain't out of your way much if you was to stop by there on the way to Wepo Wash, he thought. *That's a right fair trail that slants up the rise ahead to the top of the mesa, and it might be there's some tie-up between that horse herd in the wash and the riders that's been bothering the professor.*

Bending down, Longarm picked up the single pebble he'd placed on the south side of the stones and moved it to the east. He remounted, and, instead of turning south on the trail that led along the mesa's face, rode on east, following the centuries-old trail worn by the ancestors of the Navajos and Hopis that led to the top of Black Mesa.

Now the face of the incredibly massive formation rose in narrow shelves above him, where wind and the infrequent rains and the thin winter snows had eroded the strata and exposed it in thick layers of red or tan or brown sandstone, grey porous lava rock, and, dominating all the others, the layers of black stone that gave the mesa its name. The land slanted sharply upward to the mesa's top, and its rise brought Longarm's eyes level with one of the thick layers of black. He glanced at it idly as the crowbait nag slowed down on the increasingly steep grade. Then he frowned and reined in.

Hold up a minute here, old son, he told himself, looking more closely at the glistening black expanse. *If you didn't see enough coal when you was a kid back in West-by-god-Virginia to know it when you see it out here in Arizona Territory, you better get spectacles, because your eyes're going bad! That ain't no rock you're looking at. It's a damned rich seam of coal!*

Just to make sure he was right, Longarm dismounted and took his time walking along the trail beside the thick black layer. He took out his pocketknife and stopped now and then to pry a chip off the seam's face and crush the chip between two stones. The granules that resulted he lighted, and as he watched the oily smoke that rose from the little piles, Longarm was convinced that he was right.

Returning to his horse, he took from his saddlebag the map that had been given him by Armbruster at the Indian Bureau headquarters in Winslow. Using his thumbnail as a ruler, he measured the face of Black Mesa, from the north edge where he now stood to the end of the south face at First Mesa where it began at Polacca Wash. Allowing for the deep convolutions formed by the three protruding fingers of the subsidiary mesas, he saw that the face covered a span of almost a hundred miles.

This mesa comes close to being as big as the whole damned state of West Virginia, old son, Longarm mused. *Which all adds up to one hell of a lot of coal, even if the seams don't run back real deep. And until they begun to peter out about the time I pulled my tail off to the War, the coal mines in West Virginia made that whole state rich. Wonder if the Hopis and the Navajos know they're walking around on top of more money than they ever dreamed was in the world?*

Frowning thoughtfully, Longarm folded the map and put it back in his saddlebag. He swung onto the crowbait and rode on, shaking his head from time to time as he looked at the rich black seams that formed the mesa's face.

By the time Longarm reached the top of the mesa, the day was in its final hours. Before leaving the trail that stretched on to the east over the high desert, he stopped long enough to place a second marker which would tell Tosih Nez and Pen-tawi that he had turned and started across

135

the top of the mesa going south. Then he oriented himself by the position of the low-hanging sun and rode toward Professor Cranborn's camp.

On the mesa's top the terrain was smooth and level compared to that stretching from its base. There were no high crags, though the land rose and fell irregularly; no wide canyons or arroyos to skirt, only sparsely grassed level land with stands of stunted mountain cedar and juniper and, in the saucer-shaped depressions that occurred now and then, clumps of sagebrush.

Longarm made good progress. A ride of a little more than an hour brought him to the spot where camp had been. The pole-and-brush shelters the Navajos had erected for themselves at one side of the tent were still standing. The tent and rope corral were gone, and as far as Longarm could see there was no sign of life in any direction from the deserted campsite. Lighting a fresh cheroot, Longarm surveyed the deserted flat.

Either them night riders come back and she got so spooked she just up and left, or she's moved on to do her digging someplace else, he told himself. *Whichever way it was, she ain't here no longer, so there ain't no reason for dilly-dallying around. Just push on and by nightfall you'll be where you're headed for anyhow. If that Indian Bureau map is right, Wepo Wash heads up not more'n eight or ten miles from where you're at right now.*

To save Tosih Nez and Pen-tawi the time they might spend investigating the deserted campsite, Longarm stayed long enough to erect another miniature cairn, this one five stones high, in the center of the campsite, where the tent had stood. He placed the pebble that marked his direction on the south side of the cairn, and started for the head of Wepo Wash.

Twilight lasted longer on the top of Black Mesa than it did on the low ground that descended from the mesa's foot to the Little Colorado River. Though the last thin sliver of the sun's red disc had vanished long ago below the distant rim of the Coconino Plateau west of the river, the sky above the mesa stayed light.

Longarm had no pinpoint as his destination, and touched

the reins only to keep the horse moving south after the animal had plodded around one of the rock outcrops that broke the surface in long low ledges, or the flattened cone of a small hill, or one of the narrow creases of a cut that was not deep enough or wide enough to be called an arroyo or a canyon.

Wepo Wash was farther than he'd thought from glancing at the map. The sky had darkened to the soft, deep blue that warned that nightfall would be coming soon when Longarm saw the winding gap ahead that told him he had almost reached his objective. He let the crowbait get close to the edge of the gash before reining in, and to stretch his legs as much as to avoid showing a high silhouette against the skyline, walked up to the crevasse.

Below him the wash lay exposed. Created by the rains which fell so infrequently on that arid land, Wepo Wash was typical of the others that abounded in the area. It was in essence the dry bed of a river that flowed only after a rain.

From the edge where Longarm stood and halfway to the wide line of rocks that covered its bottom, the sides of the wash sloped gradually and were dotted with sagebrush that grew amid a thin covering of prairie grass. Beyond the ragged line where the sagebrush ended the sides plunged at a sharper angle and the ground bore a thicker coating of grass. Then there was a strip of bare earth, seamed and cut by water currents, and below the raw soil the bottom of the wash was lined with light-colored rocks that ranged in size from gravel through fist-sized stones to boulders as big as a horse.

Though the wash ran generally from northeast to southwest, its course was far from straight. Where there was a boulder too big to be rolled by the brown water that flowed down its bed after a heavy rain, or an outcrop of stone in its sloping walls that diverted the water's downhill rush, curves and even zigzags had been formed. Such a curve occurred a mile or so from where Longarm had stopped, and he remounted and rode parallel to the rim to see what lay beyond it.

In full daylight, Longarm might have passed by the gash

of a wide arroyo that ran off the bed of the wash, but in the gathering darkness the flicker of a fire in the mouth of the arroyo caught his eyes at once. Dismounting, he left the horse standing and walked along the wash's rim until he could look up the arroyo. He saw silhouetted against the fire the dark figure of a man squatting by the flames, his back to the wash. Deeper in the arroyo there was the white square of a tarpaulin supported by corner poles. He was edging closer for a better look when the voice of a woman reached him through the still air.

"I do wish you'd hurry with that food if you intend to share it with me," she said. "I'm sure you're aware that I've had nothing since breakfast, and I'm completely famished."

Longarm could not see the woman, but there was no mistaking the voice. The speaker was Professor R. M. Cranborn.

Chapter 16

On hearing Professor Cranborn's voice from the arroyo, Longarm's experience told him to hold his position, where he could both see and hear what was happening. While the professor was still speaking he dropped to the ground, for he knew that slight movements on high places are easily seen from a distance even in failing light. He'd learned of the tricks played with acoustics by the wind currents that prevailed in stony Western canyons, where moving only a step or two might make a distant sound inaudible. Lying prone on the lip of the broad wash, he listened.

"I'll feed you supper when I get around to it," the man at the fire replied to the professor.

"I must tell you that you are the most inconsiderate individual it has ever been my misfortune to encounter," the professor observed. "And I still cannot understand why you've thought it necessary to detain me."

"Listen, lady, you better be glad you're alive instead of bellyaching," the man retorted. "If you don't close up that flapping jaw you got, I'll close it for you!"

"Why do you object to my speaking out?" she asked. "No one could possibly hear me in this isolated place."

"I can hear you, and that's plenty. Now, shut that mouth of yours before I get riled any worse'n I am."

"I shall certainly report this outrage to the nearest British Consul when I return to civilization again," Professor Cranborn said tartly. "Her Majesty does not tolerate her loyal subjects being treated in this fashion."

"That's too damn bad!" the man snapped.

There was a long silence from the arroyo. Dusk was rapidly settling into darkness, and Longarm thought it safe now to lift his head and watch. He looked up in time to see the man at the fire stand up, pick up a skillet from the coals at the fire's edge, and start back to the improvised shelter. Once the man had left the wan, small circle of light cast by the fire, all that Longarm could see was the shadow he cast on the ground ahead of him, and even that disappeared when he went under the tarpaulin.

Longarm heard him say, "Here's some grub for you. I sure hope you ain't figured out how to talk and eat at the same time."

"And I hope it has occurred to even one of your mediocre mentality that it will be necessary for you to free my hands in order for me to eat," the professor retorted icily.

"If you're asking am I going to untie you, I am—long enough for you to stow your vittles away."

"I should also like to perform certain necessary natural functions, preferably before eating."

"You mean you got to go?"

"I am sure you understood what I meant. I will not allow you to force me to sink to your level of vulgarity."

"All right. But I'll have to go along with you so you don't try anything funny, like getting away."

"That is totally unnecessary, my good man. I give you my word that I will not do what you call 'anything funny.' I realize that it would be foolhardy for me to try to escape afoot, in the dark and over unfamiliar terrain."

"By God, for all that fancy talk you throw, you got more sense than I figured. Go on up the canyon a little ways and find a rock to squat behind. Just be sure you find a place short of that draw where we got the horse herd. Them wild mustangs gets spooky this time of the evening. I'll keep my eye on you, and it won't bother me a damn bit to shoot you if you try to run."

When he heard the guard mention a herd of wild mustangs, Longarm silently congratulated himself. *Looks like you found what you was looking for, old son, even if you can't take all the credit for it. There's still a lot of questions you got to find the answers for. From what old Mumu-ri-wu said, there's more'n just that one man around here somewhere, and you ain't seen hide nor hair of the horses yet, so you don't know what you're up against. But you're halfway there, anyhow.*

Through the gloom, Longarm saw a vague figure appear beyond the shelter and go a short distance up the arroyo. He was sure from the conversation he'd just heard that it was Professor Cranborn. He watched while the dimly visible form went a short distance from the shelter and disappeared, then after a few moments reappeared and returned to vanish from view again under the shelter.

Now, that poor lady's got herself into a real fix, old son, Longarm thought while he waited for something else to happen in the arroyo. *But it'd be a lot worse if there was more than one man over there, and if you hadn't happened by just now. It won't be no trick at all to sneak across after that fellow goes to sleep and take care of him. Then all there is to it is waiting till the rest of the bunch shows up and getting 'em tied down, and after that you can maybe find out what in hell is going on around here.*

Longarm's silent colloquy with himself was interrupted by the voice of the guard. "All right," he said. "You've had your supper, so I might as well fix you up for the night."

"I would suggest that you devise a more satisfactory method of securing me than you did last night," Professor Cranborn said. "I was uncomfortable, really quite uncomfortable, and I slept very badly indeed."

"You better be glad that's all you had to worry about. Lay down on that blanket now, like you was last night. I can't figure no better way than to tie your hands to the corner pole and lash your feet together. It held you last night, so I figure it'll do as good tonight. Go on—do what I told you to."

Silence followed the guard's orders, but the stillness lasted only for a few moments. From far down Wepo Wash the thudding of hoofbeats sounded, growing steadily louder.

Longarm listened carefully. It took only a few moments for his keen ears to isolate the different rhythms that told him three riders were arriving. In order to see the arroyo more clearly he sat up Indian-style, his feet crossed at the ankles. The moon had not yet risen, so he did not have to worry about being seen.

Either the guard had finished tying up Professor Cranborn or else he had heard the hoofbeats, too, for he came out of the shelter soon after Longarm first heard them and carefully placed two fresh sticks of wood on the dying fire. They blazed up and Longarm dropped flat again. The hoofbeats were very close now. The riders were keeping to the top shoulder of the wash, avoiding the treacherous footing that the wide swath of loose rock on its floor provided. They came out of the darkness into the light of the replenished fire, reining in as their mounts set their hind legs to descend to the mouth of the arroyo.

"It sure as hell taken you long enough, Slick," the guard greeted the first man who dismounted.

"Ah, shit! We had to wait while a bunch of Navajos done some swapping. There's always as many goddamn Indians around Hubbell's trading post as you'll find in one of them pueblos where they live. Fact is, I think old man Hubbell's got some redskin blood in him, he gets along with 'em so good."

"Yeah. Then we had to circle around when we left Hubbell's place so nobody'd know which way we was really heading," another of the new arrivals added.

"Anyhow, we got enough decent grub now to hold us till the job's over with," the third man said.

"And I got your chewin' plug, Blaze," the man called Slick said, handing a small package to the guard. "Even carried it in my pocket so's you wouldn't have to wait while we unloaded the packs." He jerked a thumb toward the shelter. "The dame give you any trouble?"

"Nothing but a lot of jawing," Blaze said around the bite of tobacco he'd chewed off the plug. "I'll be damn glad when—"

"Shut up!" Slick interrupted. "She can hear everything we say above a whisper."

Lowering his voice, Blaze asked, "Well, that don't matter, does it? Ain't we gonna get rid of her before we leave?"

"Sure. But if something should happen and she got loose,

142

she could put a noose around our necks."

"Yeah. I can see that. And you ain't changed your mind about us all having a crack at her before we put her away?"

"No," Slick replied. "She's awful lean and scrawny, but any woman looks good when you been stuck out here as long as we have. When we've had our fun we'll leave her for buzzard bait—but that'll be the last thing we do."

"You got it all figured out, ain't you?"

"Yep. That's the way I run a job. I figure it out first."

"Sure," Blaze agreed. "I guess a man can't be too careful."

Longarm was not surprised. After he'd seen the setup in the arroyo, he'd understood that Professor Cranborn would not be allowed to leave alive after having seen the gang's faces and overhearing their conversation during her captivity.

While Blaze and Slick talked, the other new arrivals had been taking the packs off the rumps of their horses. One of them asked, "You hungry, Blaze? We got plenty to eat now."

"Oh, I scrapped up some supper, Clem. But it'll be right good to have bacon and spuds for breakfast again instead of hottened-up beans and not even any coffee to go with 'em."

"You better tell Blaze what the boss said," the third man who'd ridden in suggested.

"You got word, then?" Blaze asked Slick.

"Yep. One reason we're so late is because that damn Hopi renegade didn't show up when he was supposed to. Three more days and we run them mustangs down the wash and turn 'em loose."

"From what he said, that renegade Hopi's been real busy, going around to all of their towns and bad-mouthing the Navajos, saying they're about to steal Hopi grass," Clem put in.

"Yeah," the other man, whose name Longarm hadn't yet heard, added. "And he claims he's got a bunch of real Navajo-haters primed to bust up a few of their houses along the edge of the Hopis' land."

Slick said confidently, "There'll be troops in here before

143

a month's out, after the fighting starts."

"You sure those Navajos are going to fight?" the third man who'd ridden in asked.

"Damn it, Fred, quit worrying!" Clem said. "That's all me and Slick heard from you on the way back—wondering what the damn Navajos was going to do!"

"You're damn right they'll fight!" Slick snapped. "At least, the boss is sure they will, and he should know."

"I guess," Fred said. "Well, damn it, I feel like I been drug through a knothole backwards. That place old Hubbell runs is just about two hours more'n a comfortable day's ride. I'm ready to get in my blankets."

"That's the smartest thing you've said tonight," Clem told him. "Soon as we get these horses up in the cut with the others we'll all turn in."

Longarm watched while Fred and Clem led the horses away from the fire and disappeared into the darkness up the arroyo. A few moments after they'd led the saddle horses out of sight, a few scattered whinnies and snorts came from the darkness. From the remark Blaze had made to the professor earlier, Longarm had already deduced that a smaller arroyo must run off the main one, and that it must be the cut mentioned by Clem. He imagined they had rigged a lariat or two across the mouth of it to keep the mustangs penned in.

A light cold wind had begun drifting down the wash and, secure from observation now, Longarm stood up and went to his horse. Untying the saddle strings that held his bedroll with his coat rolled around it, he shook out the coat and slid his arms into it. He still had a long time to wait before the outlaw camp settled down.

For the past half-hour his stomach had been sending him hints that it was uncomfortably empty. Longarm took his rations of venison jerky and parched corn out of his saddlebags and settled down again at the spot where he'd been watching the gang. With his pocketknife he shaved thin slivers of hard jerky from the two-finger-sized piece he'd selected and chewed the shaved-off shreds with grains of the corn. The corn was as hard as the jerky, and even the small mouthfuls he took required a lot of chewing. Longarm took his time. He had a while to wait, and he was in no hurry.

Apparently, the outlaws had talked out their store of conversation. They said little while they brought their bedrolls out of the tarpaulin-topped shelter and spread them around the fire. Yawning and stretching, they settled down for the night.

Since the return of the trio bringing supplies, the fire had not been replenished. It was fading now to a circle of red coals with only an occasional fugitive flame flickering up to throw out a bright burst of light. Longarm waited until the men in their bedrolls had stopped shifting around in search of the most comfortable positions, and had stopped exchanging even an occasional few words. The fire faded still more while he waited, and when only a red dot here and there indicated an active coal, he moved.

His silent, almost motionless vigil had stiffened Longarm's muscles. His mouth was dry after having eaten the jerky and corn and he wanted a cigar. He walked back to his horse and took a swallow from his canteen before leading the animal slowly away from the edge of the wash. He kept a firm hand on the bridle and let it take only a step or two at a time.

A hundred yards from the wash he found a rock outcrop high enough to hide the horse. He dropped its reins over its head and weighted the leathers with a large stone. Lighting a cheroot, he walked back and forth behind the outcrop, working the stiffness out of his muscles, his mind busy with plans for the next few hours.

You'll need to move spry, old son. It'll be moonrise in two hours, give or take a few minutes, and you got to move in on the sons of bitches while it's still dark. In this country a full moon makes things damn near as bright as daylight. Get the professor outa the way first. She ain't going to be no help taking care of them outlaw bastards, and it's more'n likely she's heard enough to be a good witness if this case ever goes to court. If she gets in the clear without rousing them, the rest of it ought not to be too hard to handle.

Longarm began his move. He decided to leave his rifle with the horse. There wasn't likely to be the need for any long-range shooting, he thought, and the rifle would just be in his way. He emptied a box of .44 cartridges for his Colt into a coat pocket, took one more swallow of water from his canteen, and ground out the butt of his cheroot on the hard ground. Then he started for Wepo Wash, picking his way carefully through the darkness.

Reaching the edge of the wide, stone-bottomed gully, he stopped for a minute opposite the mouth of the arroyo, studying the outlaw camp. The fire had died completely now, but Longarm's eyes had long ago adjusted fully to the darkness. By the starshine he could see the oblongs made by the blanket-covered sleeping men. Beyond them the square of the tarpaulin shelter made a light patch against the darker ground.

It'd sure be nice if you knew which side of that arroyo the cut with the horses in it was on, he thought. *And how far it is from the mouth. If you could get past them bastards by pussy-footing along the rim over their heads, they wouldn't be as likely to hear you. But it ain't in the cards to take a chance on spooking them wild mustangs. That'd bring them four outa their blankets in a hurry. So seeing the next best is the only choice you got, you might as well get on with it.*

Picking his way with utmost care, Longarm started down the sloping side of Wepo Wash. He walked Indian-style, taking short steps, lifting each foot straight up and planting it straight down in turn, making sure that his bootsole was on firm ground before putting his full weight on it.

Descending the gentle grade of the first part of the slope was no job at all. After he'd reached the normal high water line, where after-rain flooding had scoured the bed to a steeper angle, the going was not so easy. The soil was looser here, and the slanted ground treacherous. Leaning back, keeping his body carefully erect, Longarm took his time going down, but at last the rock-strewn bed was only a step away.

There was a gravel deposit between the soil of the bank and the stone-covered bed of the wash. The stretch of gravel was not wide, but to keep it from crunching underfoot Longarm had to lift one foot while balancing on the other, advance the foot a few inches, and lean forward slowly, letting his weight down bit by careful bit.

The most treacherous part lay ahead. The boulders that covered the bed of the wash were of all shapes and sizes. It was impossible for Longarm to see what lay ahead, and he felt his way with even greater care than he'd used when crossing the gravel. But even with all his care, there were times when a round rock or one resting on an edge would give way as it took his weight, and pull him forward or throw him to one side, forcing him to flail his arms wildly to keep his balance.

When he'd gone a step or two past the center of the wash, Longarm stopped to rest his legs for a moment before tackling the remainder of the crossing. In this section of the bottom, almost all the smaller stones had been tumbled to the sides. Here the very weight of the boulders kept them anchored in the earth. The smallest of the boulders that lined the swath where he stood was as large as a man's head, the biggest as large as a man, and Longarm had stopped to rest on one of the largest.

Ready to move on, Longarm put his foot on the round boulder that lay just ahead of him. His bootsole began to slip on its high-arched top, and he threw himself backward to keep from falling. Transferring the full weight of his body to one foot disturbed the balance of the huge stone on which he'd stopped. It began to tilt, and his foot started to skid sideways.

Longarm swung his arms, trying to hold his footing on the slowly tilting stone long enough to bring down the foot that was in the air. The stone stopped with a sudden jolt. Small as the jar was, it knocked Longarm's bootsole loose. His foot slid to the side. For a fraction of a second he swayed from one side to the other, but was unable to regain his balance.

He fell back and his head crashed down on the edge of an upthrust stone. Longarm felt the first sharp pain of impact as his head hit the boulder's edge, and then he knew nothing more.

Chapter 17

Longarm came out of a black world to find himself suspended in a sea of red. His head was throbbing in time with his heartbeats and a red film veiled his eyes, but he did not think of opening them. All his attention was absorbed in trying to connect the color he saw with the pain in his head. The film that veiled his eyes slowly faded to a dim pink, but its color kept changing with each pulsing throb. He started to rub his eyes and his aching head, but when he moved his right hand his left hand twitched and pulled the right to a halt. Again and again, Longarm willed his right arm to move, and was irritated that the arm did not obey.

Suddenly, he realized that he could open his eyes and did so. His last memory was of moving through the night, and he was surprised to find that it was full daylight. The pink film that had been fogging his vision vanished when the light struck his pupils, and with its going the gaps in his memory were closed. He suddenly remembered everything that had happened up to the time when he felt the sensation of falling and receiving a hard, painful blow on his head.

"I'm very pleased that you're finally regaining consciousness, Marshal Long," Professor Cranborn said.

Although she spoke in a whisper, her voice seemed to be right in Longarm's ear, and he started involuntarily. He turned his head in the direction of her voice. The Englishwoman was tied between two poles of the tarpaulin shelter, her hands pulled above her head and lashed to one, the rope around her ankles extended to secure her feet to the pole at the opposite corner.

Longarm was tied in the same fashion. His wrists were bound to the same support pole to which hers were tied. Their bodies lay at right angles, their heads only inches apart. He looked toward the wash. The four outlaws were lounging on the ground around the ashes where the campfire had burned the previous night.

"Are you all right, Marshal Long?" the professor asked. "I'm sure you must still be a bit dazed or you'd have replied."

"I guess I'm as all right as could be expected. My head's sure sore as hell—begging your pardon for swearing, ma'am."

"I use profanity myself on occasion," she said. "And I don't wonder that your head hurts. You have an exceedingly large contused area on the anterior temporal hemisphere."

"If you mean a bump, that's where I must've hit my head on a rock when I fell down out there in the wash." Longarm looked at the small thin triangle of sky visible at the head of the arroyo and asked, "What time of day is it?"

"They brought me food quite a while ago, so it must be the middle of the afternoon."

"Just curious. The way I feel, I've been out quite a while."

"You have. I don't know what the time was when those men brought you here, but it was in the middle of the night. You were so limp that until they began talking about killing you—finishing you off, they called it—I thought you were dead."

"I ain't quite that far gone yet," Longarm told her, his voice grim.

He continued taking stock of his situation. He was lying on his back, and his coat had been removed, but not his vest. His watch chain was gone, and he realized that one of his captors must have taken the watch and the derringer that was attached to the other end of the chain. His gunbelt had also been removed.

Professor Cranborn asked, "What actually happened,

149

Marshal? I'm still quite at a loss to understand how they captured you."

"I stumbled onto their camp about dark, and when I saw you, I figured I better get you away from 'em. I was walking across the wash when my foot slipped and my head hit something. That must've been when they heard me."

"You were coming to rescue me? I'm—well, I'm tremendously touched, and I thank you most sincerely."

"I was just doing what my job calls for, Professor. I don't look for special thanks. But go on and tell me what else the outlaws said while I was out."

"As I just said, they discussed killing you. Then they decided to wait and kill us both just before they leave. I received quite a surprise while I was listening to them. It seems that they captured me for the sole purpose of murdering me."

"You must've figured out from what they said that they were the night riders you told me about."

"Yes, I made the connection at once."

"Well, they were afraid you'd seen their faces. They knew if they got caught you could identify 'em and be a witness against 'em, testify in court who they was."

"To be sure. That had not occurred to me, Marshal."

"You better not keep on calling me that, Professor," Longarm told her. "It's just going to remind the outlaws that I'm a lawman, and that'll keep 'em all riled up."

"What shall I call you, then?"

"I got a sorta nickname my friends use. Longarm."

"Longarm," the professor repeated reflectively. "Yes, of course, I see the derivation. If I am to address you familiarly, then you must do the same thing. My full name is Rebecca Mary Cranborn. However, my friends call me Becky."

"All right, Becky." Longarm nodded. "Looks like we're in a mess together, but don't worry. We'll get out of it all right."

"You sound very sure. I must admit, Longarm, that I feel better now that I have company. I've been feeling quite alone since those men brought me here."

"How'd they come to capture you, anyhow?"

"I gathered from their discussions before you arrived that

they are in the process of committing some crime. Until you mentioned it, I didn't think of myself as being a threat to them."

"You hadn't seen 'em doing anything, had you?"

"Of course not! However, with my camp so near here, they must have been afraid I had seen them in some kind of criminal activity while I was what they called snooping around."

"What happened to the Navajos you had at your camp? Didn't they try to help you?"

"No. Of course, the outlaws—that is what you call them here in the States, isn't it?" Longarm nodded and she went on, "The outlaws had no way of knowing that I had absolutely no interest in them. I had no idea they were in the vicinity until they came to my camp just at daylight and threatened my workers with rifles. I can't say I blame the Indians for leaving as they were ordered to."

"When was that?"

"Two—no, three days ago."

"A minute ago you said they been talking pretty free since they brought you here. Was any of their talk about the horse herd they're holding up there towards the back of the arroyo?"

"They've mentioned turning the horses loose. Actually, they've had very little to say about anything except the jolly good time they plan to have later."

"You heard any names mentioned?"

"Only the names they call one another. Slick and Clem and Blaze and Fred. I would imagine that Slick and Blaze are *noms de guerre*."

"I guess I don't follow that word you used."

"A French phrase for alias, Longarm."

"I see." Longarm looked back at the outlaws. "There's a wanted flyer out on a train robber. His real name's Alonzo Pratt, but the flyer says he travels under the name of Slick, if I recall rightly. I ain't got a thing to go by on the others."

"I've noticed they aren't especially friendly toward one another, though the two called Slick and Blaze do seem to be on somewhat better terms than the others."

"Well, their names don't matter much right now. What

151

I got to do first of all is figure out how to get loose, and get my hands on a gun."

"Do I understand your intention correctly, Longarm? Are you thinking of escaping?"

"I aim to make a pretty good stab at it, Becky."

"If it will help you any, your revolver is lying beside my Purdey, on the other side of this fly."

By craning his neck at an awkwardly painful angle, Longarm found that he could see the weapons. There were also four rifles, which he guessed belonged to their captors, lying along the edge of the shelter at right angles to his feet.

"You didn't get a chance to use your shotgun?" he asked.

"There would be at least one less outlaw here if I had," Becky said grimly. "But they took me totally unawares."

"All I got to do," Longarm went on, more to himself than to his companion, "is to get my hands free and grab one of the guns before they know I'm loose."

"May I assume that your plans include freeing me?"

"Why sure. I'd see you're safe before I tackle the outlaws. You can bet your bottom dollar on that."

"What can I do to help you?"

"I don't know right now. But give me a little time to figure, and I'll try to come up with some sort of scheme."

Longarm fell silent, and though Becky continued to watch him, she did not speak. He glanced first at the four outlaws, who were still lounging beside the ashes of the dead fire. They were engrossed in whatever topic they were discussing and paying no attention to the prisoners.

Craning his neck and twisting his head again, Longarm studied the bindings that held his feet. Two strands of manila rope had been formed into a figure eight to pull his ankles together. Then the rope had been brought up between his legs and pulled tight before being stretched to the corner of the tarpaulin shelter and tied to the supporting pole. Before turning his attention to the lashings on his wrists, he looked at Becky's feet and saw that she had been tied in the same manner.

Half-inch-wide strips of rawhide had been used to tie his wrists. Each wrist was tied separately with a double slip-knot which pulled them together, and the ends of the strips were then tied to the support pole. There was a six-inch length of rawhide between his lashed wrists and the pole. Longarm tested the binding by pulling, but only succeeded in tightening the loops around his wrists. Again, Becky had been bound in the same way, but her hands had been tied a few inches lower on the pole than his. The vague outline of the plan that had begun forming in his mind took on a more definite shape.

He glanced at the outlaws again. Slick was on his feet now, his companions were getting up, and their talk seemed about at an end. Longarm frowned. He needed time to think and time to work, and he was prepared to buy it at any cost.

"Looks to me like they're starting to stir," he warned Becky. "Don't let on like we've been talking, and don't talk to me no more'n you got to while they're around. Act like you're too put out to notice them or me or anything else."

"It would help if you—"

Longarm interrupted her. "I ain't got time to explain right now, Becky. They're coming up here. Just keep your eyes open and your mouth shut, like I asked you to."

"Very well. Even if I don't understand, you can rely on my discretion."

Still keeping his eyes on the group at the mouth of the arroyo, he said, "Sure. Don't worry, neither. We'll get outa this mess sooner or later."

A glance showed Longarm that the outlaws were all on their feet now. Watching them covertly, he saw them start toward the shelter. He closed his eyes and let himself relax. In a moment he heard the approaching footsteps of the outlaws grinding on the hard soil. The grating noises stopped as the four reached the tarpaulin shelter.

"Damned if the son of a bitch ain't still out," one of them said. Longarm recognized the voice of Blaze.

"He taken a hell of a whack on his head," Clem said.

"It wasn't all that hard." This was Slick's voice. "I think the bastard's playing possum."

Longarm felt a boot-toe prodding his ribs. He'd decided there was nothing to be gained by trying to deceive them, and opened his eyes. In the foreshortened perspective forced

153

on him by his position, the four outlaws towered above him like giants.

"Looks like we caught us a live one," Slick grinned.

"I'd just as soon he wasn't, Slick," Blaze growled. "Too bad he didn't crack his thick skull wide open when he hit them rocks last night. It'd've served him right."

"It won't be any trouble to get rid of him when we're ready to pull out," Slick said. He reached into his pocket and took out Longarm's wallet, and flipped it open to expose the badge pinned inside. "Deputy U. S. Marshal C. Long," he read from the face of the badge. "You're the one they call Longarm, I guess?"

"I been called that," Longarm admitted. "And you'd be a low-living piece of scum named Alonzo Pratt."

Slick's face twisted angrily, then smoothed into a smug grin. "How'd you know that?" he asked. "We ain't never crossed paths before."

Knowing the risk he took, Longarm went on with his quickly formed plan. He knew he had little time in which to work, and the success of what he intended to do depended on drawing the outlaws off balance, clouding their judgment by rousing their anger. The outlaws were already on edge; he'd noted that while listening to their talk the night before. His job now was to draw that edge finer without crossing the dangerous line that would trigger them into violent action against their prisoners.

In a calm, matter-of-fact voice, Longarm replied, "Oh, we try to keep track of the small-time crooks as well as the big ones, Alonzo. You ain't important enough for us Federal marshals to waste our time on. We leave the penny-ante players like you and your friends to constables and sheriffs."

"You knew my name right away," Slick retorted. He dug into his pocket again and produced Longarm's watch and derringer. "There'll be a lot more who'll know it when word gets around I'm the man that finished off the famous Longarm with his own gun."

"Nobody's been able to say that so far," Longarm told him, unruffled. "And you won't live to say it, either."

Slick bent over and thrust the muzzle of the derringer into Longarm's temple. "Don't bet on it. I can pull this trigger any time I feel like it."

"Wait a minute, Slick!" Blaze protested. "You was giving me hell last night because I talked about doing something you hadn't planned. Now, you just got through telling us the last thing we'd do before we pull outa here is take care of him and the woman. How come you can change your mind and we can't?"

"Yeah," Clem chimed in. "Don't seem to me like all the jawing you been doing about how we got to do what you say means a hell of a lot. Not if you can just do what you feel like."

"Shut up!" Slick snapped. "Until the boss changes things, I'm still in charge here." Nevertheless, he contented himself with turning back to Longarm and saying, "Big talk won't buy you anything this time, Longarm. And I guess it'll hurt you more to lay there and think about what you're going to get than it would if I put you outa your misery now."

Without raising his voice, Longarm said, "You ain't man enough to do that, Pratt. And neither are them saddle tramps you're pushing around. All any of you is fit for is what you're doing right now: playing nursemaid to a bunch of mangy mustangs."

"Come on, let's get out of here," Slick said. "He'll find out soon enough that he's finally played out his string."

When the four outlaws had walked back to the mouth of the arroyo, Becky said, "If whatever you plan to do includes irritating them, I'd say you have succeeded."

"I ain't got all that much of a plan yet, Becky," Longarm confessed. "Right now, I'm just trying to get that Slick Pratt so riled up that he can't think straight himself and he'll tell the others to leave us alone."

"You're not ready to talk about your idea yet?"

"No. I still got to scheme a little bit more. But just in case, we better rest all we can right now, because if what I got in mind works out right, we'll need to be ready."

During the tag-end of the afternoon that remained, Longarm and Becky talked little. Longarm tested his bonds several times, but did not dare carry his testing too far. He expected them to be checked before the day ended, and creating slack prematurely would be wasted effort. When

155

not dozing, he and Becky watched their captors, who did nothing except sit at the mouth of the arroyo and play cards until just before sunset, when they built a small fire and cooked supper.

Fred and Clem, obviously under orders not to talk to the prisoners, brought tin plates of greasy fried potatoes and fat bacon to the shelter and fed Longarm and Becky, untying only their right hands to allow them to eat. As Longarm had expected, the two men checked the ropes and rawhide thongs before leaving. They rejoined Slick and Blaze, and as the sun dropped, darkening the side of the arroyo with the deep shadow cast by its high wall, the four outlaws replenished the fire and resumed their card game.

"Let's get started," Longarm said. "They can't see any too good when they look away from the fire."

"What do you want me to do?" Becky asked.

"Nothing till I get a foot worked free. These fellows never learned how to tie a man up. They didn't have sense enough to take off my boots, so I got a little slack to work on."

Longarm tensed his muscles and bent his knee. He rotated his foot and straightened his ankle, bringing his powerful thigh muscles into play. A quarter of an hour passed before he felt his heel slip past the rope and pop free. After that, getting the other foot free was a simple matter of shaking off the loose loop of the figure-eight tie.

"Good show!" Becky whispered when Longarm rolled on his side, both feet freed from their bonds. "But your hands—"

"That's where you got to help me, Becky. I got to ask you to do something that might—"

"Don't worry about what I might think, Longarm," she broke in. "Just tell me what has to be done."

"Like I said, these fellows don't know how to tie a man, and they used rawhide on our wrists because it'll pull tighter. They never stopped to think that rawhide stretches when it gets wet."

"But how are you going to wet it?"

"Only one way I know. I got to pee on it."

"Oh." Becky paused, then asked, "What you want me to do is to direct the stream?"

"That's about the size of it. You don't mind, do you?"

"I meant it when I told you I'd do anything Longarm," Becky said firmly. "Stop apologizing and tell me how to start."

Chapter 18

"I've got to twist myself around to where you can reach me first," Longarm said. "I studied and studied while I was trying to figure out the best way. I can't do it myself with my hands tied like they are. Let's see if I got it worked out."

Longarm turned on his side and used his feet to propel his body until he lay beside Becky. He brought his legs up and bent at the waist, he arms stretched to the utmost, until his crotch was within reach of her fingers.

"Can you reach my pants buttons now?" he asked.

Her voice showing the effort she was making, Becky said, "If you can bend your back just a little more, I'll be able to." Longarm strained to jack-knife his body further. Becky told him, "You'll have to push closer to me, Longarm. Just an inch or two, and I can reach you." Longarm squeezed out the extra effort and his hip dragged the ground as he gained the needed inch. She said, "Now stay right there. My fingers are so clumsy, with my hands tied this way—"

Longarm felt her hands working at his fly. "It feels to me like you're doing all right," he told her.

"Yes. I can..." Becky hesitated for a moment, then asked, "Are you ready for me to—to take your member out?"

"Any time." In his strained position, Longarm could not see what Becky was doing, but he felt her hands on him, tugging.

"I don't think this is going to work, Longarm," she said after a moment had gone by. "You're still too far from the knots to reach them with a stream."

"Wait a minute. I'll rear up till I can dribble down on my wrists." He elbowed himself to a crouch. The strips of rawhide bit cruelly into his tightly bound wrists, but he knew he could endure it for the few minutes that would be required. He said, "Point it to the rawhide, Becky. I'm ready to let go."

Becky's hands made the necessary adjustment. Only an instant passed before she said, "Now. Whenever you're ready."

Longarm strained and in a few moments felt his urine begin to flow in a warm flood over his wrists and hands. He compressed his abdominal muscles to squeeze his bladder until it was drained and when the flow trickled away and stopped, called to Becky to release him. He dropped to the ground and stretched in grateful relief as the tension in his muscles began to ebb.

"Do you think you wet the rawhide enough?" Becky asked.

"We'll know in a minute. If we did, it'll stretch fast."

Longarm glanced through the gloom toward the arroyo's mouth. The outlaws were still engrossed in their card game. He tugged on the strips around his wrists and thought he could feel them give a bit. Folding his thumb into his palm, he concentrated on freeing his right hand. The soaked rawhide was stretching faster now, and as Longarm kept pulling against it he suddenly felt the strips relax and found that he could slide his hand free. Wasting no time, he pulled away his left hand.

"I'm loose," he announced. "And as soon as I can get my knife out of my pants pocket, you will be, too."

"You're an ingenious man, Longarm," Becky told him, watching him cut the strips away from her wrists and begin sawing at the rope that still bound her ankles. "It seemed so improbable. I hope the rest of your plan goes as smoothly."

"I ain't got much of a plan from here on," Longarm said as he hobbled to where his boot lay and pushed his foot into it. He turned to face her, realized that he was still exposed, and quickly adjusted his fly. He started for his gunbelt, lying at the side of the shelter. Over his shoulder he asked, "You think you can bring yourself to use that shotgun?"

"I'm ready to do anything else we need to, Longarm. Don't worry. I have no qualms at all about shooting those outlaws. It wouldn't be the first time I've shot vermin."

Longarm finished strapping on his gunbelt. He picked up his coat and took a handful of cartridges from the pocket. He asked Becky, "What size shot is that Purdey of yours loaded with?"

"I don't know, exactly. I'm sure you would, because they're American loads. I asked the clerk in the gunshop for something to use on large game. He called them number four buckshot. But I don't have any shells except those in the chambers."

"They'll do fine," Longarm assured her. "But remember, you only got two shots." He handed her the Purdey. "Anyhow, we won't shoot unless we have to. I'd sooner see those four standing in front of a judge than stretched out dead on the ground."

"It would be rather unsporting to shoot them without giving them a chance," Becky agreed. She broke the Purdey to check its chambers. "Father said one should never stoop to pot shooting."

Longarm stared at her incredulously while he made a final adjustment to his holster, then said, "Well, it ain't quite the same. But they've got some answers I need to close out my case."

"What shall I do, then?" she asked.

"Move as quiet as you can, Becky. You cover the two on the right-hand side of the fire and I'll take the ones on the left side. If they go for their guns when I tell 'em to put their hands up, don't waste no time pulling your trigger."

They separated a few steps away from the shelter. The sun had left the arroyo floor now, and the outlaws were still intent on their card game. They were outlined by the bright flames as Longarm and Becky began their stealthy approach.

In bright daylight, he would not have allowed Becky to go with him, but he knew that the odds at this time of day would be against the outlaws. When the men who had been facing the fire looked away from it, their eyes would not be adjusted to the shaded area in which he and Becky would be standing.

Longarm counted on being able to aim faster and more accurately than the four, who would have to wait for their pupils to expand in order to aim at a target in the twilight gloom.

Given the advantages of surprise and light, the foray made by Longarm and Becky would have been successful if the outlaw called Blaze had not dropped his chewing tobacco. As he reached to recover the fallen plug, the outlaw changed his position and saw Longarm, who was still fifty feet away.

"Look out!" Blaze yelled, clawing for his pistol butt. "That son of a bitch Longarm's got loose!"

Longarm cut Blaze down before the outlaw's gunsight cleared the holster, but the few seconds that passed between his warning shout and Longarm's shot gave the others time to react.

Slick was on the right-hand side of the fire. He dropped his cards when Blaze shouted and began rolling toward the wash. Becky blasted at him with the Purdey. Even though she'd failed to judge her lead properly and most of the buckshot only pocked the dirt where he'd been when she pulled the Purdey's trigger, Slick yelped with pain.

He jumped up and dodged as she fired the second barrel, and this time her shooting was better. Slick's leg crumpled. He went down on one knee but quickly regained his feet and ran on, limping now, until he reached the wash and dodged out of sight behind the wall of the arroyo.

Clem was sitting beside Blaze on the left side of the fire. He jumped up at Blaze's warning and started to draw, but when his companion fell and he saw Longarm's aim shifting to him, he stopped his arm in midair and cried, "Hold up, Marshal! I quit! I ain't going to get myself killed!"

Longarm held his fire. He'd heard the two booming blasts of Becky's shotgun, but had been too busy with his own problems to look in her direction. He flicked his eyes away from Clem just in time to see Becky lowering the shotgun.

Her eyes wide open, she was staring helplessly at the fourth outlaw, Fred, who was dragging his revolver from its holster.

Instantly, Longarm's Colt followed the direction of his eyes. Fred had his pistol out and was aiming it at Becky when the heavy slug from Longarm's .44 smashed into his chest. Fred crumpled to the ground. As he fell he dropped his gun forever.

Seeing Longarm's attention diverted, Clem had decided to go on with his interrupted draw. He had his weapon in his hand when from the corner of his eyes Longarm caught the flicker of the outlaw's moving arm. In one smooth, economical motion, Longarm swivelled his wrist and fired. Clem died with his finger on the trigger of his gun.

Longarm did not need to check the fallen outlaws to make sure they could do no more damage. He knew where his shots had gone. He called across the arroyo to Becky, "You all right?"

"I—yes, I am. I'm just fine, even though I'm sure this must be a bad dream of some sort."

"It ain't a dream, Becky," Longarm assured her. "Even if it was, it ain't over yet."

Feeling in the breast pocket of his coat, Longarm found that his supply of cigars had not been touched. Lighting up, he started walking across the arroyo to join Becky. As he moved, he flipped open the Colt's cylinder and began replacing the three rounds he'd fired with fresh cartridges from his coat pocket.

"What did you mean, Longarm, that it's not over?" she asked as he came up to her.

"Don't forget that Slick's out there someplace. And, if I judge him right, he ain't the running-away kind. Chances are he's circling back here about now, figuring to finish us off."

"It's my fault he got away," Becky said. "I'm sorry I shot so poorly." She stopped, frowned, and went on, "Or perhaps I'm not. I think what I mean is that I'm sorry I was a bad shot, and I'm sorry Slick got away, but I can't bring myself to believe I'm sorry I didn't kill him."

"Be that as it may, I got to go after him."

162

"In the dark?"

Longarm looked at the sky. "I'll be able to see pretty good for almost another hour. If I don't run Slick down by then, I'll head back. If you keep the fire burning and stay back from it in the dark, you'll be safe enough."

"What about—" Becky indicated the bodies lying sprawled around the fire.

"They ain't going noplace. Slick's alive, and dangerous as a rattlesnake in the summertime."

"Just the same, if you're going to go after him and leave me here alone, I'd hate to have to watch those dead eyes staring up at me. Could we cover them up before you leave?"

"I guess there's time for that. Tell you what, Becky, you go on up to the shelter and pick me out a rifle. A Winchester, if there's one among 'em. Be sure it's got a full magazine. I'll be there as soon as I cover up them dead ones, and we'll find you a safe place to get into until I come back."

Longarm made quick work of dragging the four bodies away from the fire. He checked the guns for which the dead outlaws had no more use and found that Blake had carried a .44 S&W. After covering the bodies with the blanket on which the outlaws had been dealing cards, he built up the fire, using most of the scanty supply of firewood heaped nearby. Carrying the S&W, he went up to the shelter.

Becky ignored the pistol in Longarm's hand, but held out a rifle to him. "This looks like the best of them," she said. "I know very little about rifles, but I think the magazine is full."

Longarm checked the gun quickly. "It's all right. Now, see what you think about this, Becky. Seems to me the best place you can get is up in the little end of this arroyo, where it narrows down. Suppose you take this pistol. It's loaded, and it takes the same cartridges mine does, so here are some spare shells."

Becky took the revolver and hefted it. "I've never shot a pistol, Longarm."

"If you can shoot a shotgun, you can shoot a pistol. This one's a double-action. That means all you got to do is pull the trigger when you want to fire it."

"But what if Slick—"

"Chances are he's holed up close by. He was hit in the leg, so he can't move fast or get far. And he's left a blood trail for me to follow."

"Longarm, suppose—"

"Don't go supposing. I ain't going all that far off. When it gets too dark to see, I'll come on back here."

Becky sighed. Her voice betraying her reluctance, she said, "You've been right so far, and I'm sure you are now. Go on, then, Longarm. But hurry back."

"I'll walk up to the end of the arroyo with you and make sure you're comfortable," Longarm said. "Come on."

Side by side they started up the gulch. They'd taken only a few steps before a horse loomed in front of them, then another.

"Where on earth did they—" Becky began.

Before Longarm could explain about the mustang herd a chorus of neighs and whinnies filled the air and the arroyo in front of them was filled with horses. Longarm suddenly realized why and by whom the half-wild mustangs had been freed.

"It's Slick Pratt's work," he said. "He circled back for a horse, and now he's turned the herd loose. Come on!"

Longarm started for the mouth of the arroyo, Becky running with him. They'd only gone a few paces when he looked back and saw that they'd never make it before the mustangs ran over them. He scanned the steep walls that hemmed them in on both sides. Nowhere was there a place that slanted gently enough for them to climb. The horses behind them were moving faster now, getting a taste of freedom after having been penned up for such a long time. The leaders were beginning to gallop, forming a triangle, and behind the triangle the arroyo was filled wall to wall with a horses, their sharp-edged hooves beginning to stir up fine dust from the stone-hard ground.

Just ahead, Longarm saw a massive boulder jutting out of the vertical wall. It was the nearest thing to a haven in sight. He grabbed Becky's arm and pulled her across the arroyo, angling toward the huge stone. The tempo of the tattooing hooves was louder. The bulk of the mustang herd had speeded up to a gallop, and they were near enough now for Longarm to see the whites of their wildly walling eyes.

Longarm and Becky reached the boulder instants before the first wave of the wall overwhelmed them. He shoved Becky into the angle between the huge rock and the dirt wall of the arroyo and sheltered her by standing in front of her just as the solid line of freedom-seeking horses came abreast of their shelter.

With the dust raised by the mustangs' hooves added to the twilight, visibility in the cut was reduced to a few yards. The herd was still passing when Longarm got a glimpse of Slick Pratt on the back of one of the horses. Longarm brought up the rifle and triggered it just as a mustang forced against the wall by its fellows brushed the Winchester's muzzle. The mustang reared and whinnied, but dropped back on its hooves and kept running. By that time, the outlaw had disappeared in the confused mass of bobbing rumps and streaming tails.

"What were you shooting at?" Becky asked when the tattoo of hooves on baked soil had diminished enough for them to talk.

"Slick Pratt. He's mounted and mixed up in that bunch of mustangs. Stay here where you're safe. I'm going after him!"

Longarm spoke over his shoulder as he started down the arroyo. Ignoring the straggling mustangs that still followed the bulk of the herd toward the arroyo mouth, he began running. He got almost to the place where the shelter had stood—there was nothing visible now but the backs of the milling horses—before he reached the main body of the herd. Ahead, the mustangs were pressed so closely together that he could go no farther. He looked for a place where the wall could be scaled and found one on the other side of the arroyo.

Dodging the hooves of the animals at the tail end of the herd, Longarm reached the low spot and scrambled to the rim of the cut. He saw at once why the herd had stopped. The mustangs were half wild and, like all wild animals, feared fire. When the leaders reached the blaze Longarm had recently replenished, they had begun milling, dashing back and forth in unreasoning panic. The panic had spread through the herd, and the mouth of the arroyo was blocked.

Longarm began running along the edge, his eyes searching for Slick Pratt. He was within a few yards of the wash before he saw him. The outlaw had somehow worked through the animals and reached the mouth of the arroyo. He was at the edge of Wepo Wash, and in seconds would disappear behind its high sides.

Without slowing down, Longarm brought up the Winchester and snapshot twice as fast as he could pump the loading lever. Both shots missed. He stopped and took careful aim. As his shot rang out Longarm saw two muzzle flashes across the wash, and a split second later the reports reached his ears. He saw Slick's body jerk as the slugs hit. Lowering his rifle, Longarm watched impassively as the outlaw tumbled from his saddle.

When Slick's body hit the ground and lay still, Longarm started walking toward the arroyo mouth. He'd just reached the edge of the wash when a voice he recognized hailed him from the other side. The voice was that of Tosih Nez.

"Longarm! You are all right?"

"Fine!" Longarm shouted. "Come on over!"

Standing atop the edge of the arroyo, Longarm looked down at the backs of the milling mustangs. Their panic was subsiding. The fire had been scattered as the pressure of the herd pushed the leaders into the blaze, and the horses were wandering into Wepo Wash. He started back, reached the spot where he'd climbed out, slid to the floor, and started up the arroyo to find Becky.

Chapter 19

Halfway up the arroyo Longarm met Becky. She was walking slowly through the veil of dust that still hung in the air. Longarm hurried to meet her.

"You ain't hurt, are you?" he asked.

"No. I'm still shaking from fright, but I'm all right. Did you—" She let the rest of the question hang as they walked toward the arroyo mouth.

Longarm nodded. "Slick Pratt's dead."

"You had to shoot him, I guess."

"There was three of us shot him, Becky. I don't know whose bullet got him."

"*Three* of—" Becky stared at Longarm, bewilderment on her face. "Are you mad, or am I?"

"There's a Navajo policeman and a young Hopi working on this case with me," he explained. "We got separated a while back, and they just caught up. They saw me chasing after Slick, trying to bring him down, and helped out."

"I see." With something close to a plea in her voice, she said, "Your case is closed now, isn't it?"

"Just about. There's a few loose ends I got to tie up. But now that Slick's gone, there won't be any more trouble here. You can sleep easy tonight, and go back and fix your camp up again without having a thing to worry about."

"I've decided not to go back to the mesa," Becky said. "I wouldn't have time to start my work again. I must be in England to prepare for my classes before the new college term begins."

"You mean you're a professor in a real college?"

"Of course. What did you think?"

"I guess, I *didn't* think. Well, if you ain't setting up your camp again, I guess we'll be riding into Winslow together."

"Yes. And I'll be glad to have the company. I'm sure my nerves won't return to normal for quite some time."

Longarm rebuilt the fire while they waited for Tosih Nez and Pen-tawi to cross Wepo Wash. Darkness had fallen before the two arrived, leading Longarm's horse as well as the one Slick had been riding. The outlaw's body was draped over his saddle. Tosih Nez and Pen-tawi dismounted and lifted Slick down to the ground.

"You caught up just about the right time," Longarm said, after introducing them to Becky.

"We followed your trail," Tosih Nez explained. "We had not found your footprints coming here to the arroyo when we heard you shoot. Then we saw you and—" He indicated Slick's corpse.

Becky turned her back on the body. "I think I'll walk up the arroyo while you're busy," she told them.

Longarm waited until she was out of earshot before he asked, "I don't reckon you searched him?"

"No. We had enough to do. We didn't stop for that," Tosih Nez replied.

"We'd better take a quick look in his pockets before we stack him with the others that're under that blanket, then," Longarm said. "There's somebody big behind all this— somebody who hired Slick and his cronies, and was telling them what to do. He's the one I want to get my hands on, and maybe Slick's got something on him that'll give me the lead I need."

Their search of Slick's body produced Longarm's derringer and watch and his badge in its leather wallet. When he'd tucked the badge into his pocket and restored his derringer and watch to their usual places, Longarm felt fully dressed for the first time since he'd been a prisoner. In addition to his belongings, there was surprisingly little in the pockets Longarm searched first: a small amount of cash, a half-empty sack of tobacco, and matches.

Then, from the bloodstained pocket of the outlaw's shirt,

he drew out a piece of paper. It had been torn by a bullet passing through it and was partially soaked with blood. Longarm carried the dripping paper to the fire and looked at it. Only the bottom half of the sheet was legible; the outlaw's blood had saturated the fibers of the top half so completely that it might as well have been blank. Longarm read what he could. It started in the middle of a sentence.

Navajo and Hopi start fighting, the Army will be called in and the Indians' treaty will be declared void. For your services in bringing this about, my friends in New York will pay you $1,000 in gold coin on the day the Indian Bureau takes full control of both reservations.

There was no signature.

"I do not understand." Tosih Nez frowned, gazing at the paper in Longarm's hand. "A letter should have the name of the person who wrote it."

"Not this letter," Longarm said grimly. "Whoever wrote it was too smart to sign it."

"Is there a way to read the rest of it?" Pen-tawi asked. "Maybe if you dry it by the fire . . ."

Doubt in his expression, Longarm agreed. "Maybe. We'll try it."

Finding a flat stone at the edge of the wash took only a moment or two. Longarm placed the stone beside the fire and smoothed the paper on its top, then turned to the others.

"We might as well put Slick's body with the rest of his gang," he said. "We'll bury them tomorrow. After supper, we can sit down and figure out what we got to do next. Except I'm damned if I know where we can even make a start."

They lifted the outlaw's limp body, carried it to the huddle of blanket-covered corpses that Longarm had dragged to the side of the arroyo, and placed Slick beside his companions. When the bodies had been covered again and they were starting back to the fire, Pen-tawi pointed to the rock on which Longarm had spread the blood-soaked sheet of paper.

"Look!" he exclaimed. "It burns!"

Two quick strides carried Longarm to the stone, but the sheet had been burned away before he reached the fire.

"It's gone now," Longarm said to Tosih Nez and Pen-tawi. "We can't even prove there was such a letter, let alone find the man who wrote it."

"Could men in New York remove our lands from control of the Navajo council?" Tosih Nez asked, his voice worried.

"I don't think anybody in New York could, but there are men there who can get the Indian Bureau to do just about anything they want," Longarm said.

"This is not a good thing." Tosih Nez frowned. "Life was bad for the Navajo when the Indian Bureau was ruling us."

"And for the Hopi, too," Pen-tawi chimed in. "My people would suffer with the *tuva-suh* if this thing happened."

"Why would they want our land?" Tosih Nez asked. "Look over it, Longarm! It is not good for farming or for grazing big cattle herds. It was given to us, and it is all we have. Why do others want to take it from us now?"

Longarm thought of the rich coal seams under Black Mesa and said, "I've got a pretty good idea why, Tosih Nez. And if there's anything I can do to bust up this scheme, I'll do it."

A grating of footsteps on the arroyo floor announced Becky's return. She came into the circle of firelight, carrying a torn and dirty sack.

"I hope your friends brought some food with them, Longarm," she said. "The horses trampled over most of what was at the shelter. I managed to salvage enough scraps for dinner, but that's all."

"How about it? You got any food?" Longarm asked Tosih Nez.

"Only a little. I did not tell you why we got here so late. The last day before we got to Winslow there was much rain. After we placed Mrs. Blaisdell in the jail and started back, all the washes and dry creekbeds were flooded."

"We could not cross any of them," Pen-tawi affirmed. "It was the same at Jeddito, Polacca, Oraibi, Denebitto.

170

Only Moenkopi was dry. We had to circle wide to get to Shonto."

Tosih Nez continued, "When Desiba gave us your message, we left at once to follow you. We brought no food from the trading post."

"Well, we weren't planning on staying here," Longarm said. "You did what you were supposed to—got Mae Blaisdell to jail." He paused suddenly, thought for a moment, and said, "I missed a bet when we were talking about that letter. Mae Blaisdell."

"Do you think she would—" Tosih Nez began.

Longarm interrupted him. "She might not know, or if she knows, she might balk at telling me. But I got a hunch she'd do some talking if I dangled the right bait in front of her. Only I've got to get to her before she hears about Slick and his men being dead. How far's it from here to Winslow, Tosih Nez?"

"Three days. A long day of riding to Don Lorenzo Hubbell's trading post at Ganado, and two days to Winslow."

"If I lead Slick's horse to swap off to when mine gets tired, can I make it in two days?" Longarm asked.

Tosih Nez shook his head. "I know of no one who has ridden it in less than three."

"I can try," Longarm said. He turned to Becky. "Tosih Nez and Pen-tawi are going to clean up here. Then they'll be travelling to Winslow. I guess you can ride a horse all right?"

"My dear Longarm, I was riding to hounds with the Berkshire Hunt when I was fifteen," Becky smiled.

"You don't mind going with Tosih Nez and Pen-tawi, do you?"

"No. I don't understand why you must hurry so, but—"

"Becky, the Indian brush telegraph can get word out about what's happened quicker than ours can with all of its wires. And Mae's got a lot of Indian friends. That extra day I can maybe cut off might make a lot of difference. I'm going to ride out tomorrow morning before daylight."

"I can understand that." She nodded. "Will I see you in

171

Winslow, then? I'm sure I'll need a rest for a few days after such a trip. I stored my trunk at the Harvey House when I stopped on the way up here. I suppose that's where you'll stay?"

Recalling his experience at Winslow's other hotel, Longarm nodded. "Sure. Maybe we can have supper together before you take your train."

"That would be very nice."

"I'll be looking for you, then," Longarm promised.

Bone-weary after two and a half days in the saddle, Longarm dismounted in front of the Winslow jail. He tried to dust himself off, but the layer of red desert sand was too thick.

The jail was even less impressive inside than its redstone exterior had been. A desk occupied a corner of a narrow room spanning the building's front; a corridor that had two cells on either side opened from the front room. A chubby man with almost as heavy a coating of stubble on his face as there was on Longarm's sat at the desk. Longarm walked over and displayed his badge.

"You got a prisoner of mine here," he said.

"That'd be the woman some Navajo policeman brought in? Name of Blaisdell?" When Longarm nodded, the jailer asked, "You come to take custody of her?"

"Not yet. I just want to talk to her. In private, if you can manage it."

"Well . . ." the jailer hesitated. "Seeing as she's the only one in the lockup right now, I might step across the street for a drink, if I had the price of a drink and you said you'd be responsible for the place here while I'm gone."

Longarm fished out half a dollar and laid it on the desk. "Have two or three drinks, friend. And I'll be responsible."

Mae was in one of the rear cells. She looked up sullenly when Longarm appeared. "I thought that was you I heard talking," she said. "I guess you want me to do some talking to you, or you wouldn't be here. Well, Marshal Custis Long, after the good time we had in Gallup, you played me a mighty dirty trick. I'm not talking to you or anybody else."

"I wasn't the only one who played dirty tricks, Mae," Longarm reminded her. "You're still alive after what you call my dirty trick. If yours had worked, I'd be dead now."

"I wish you were!" Mae snapped. "Get the hell out of here, Longarm! You'll get nothing from me!"

"I don't know for sure that I need much from you, Mae. You see," Longarm went on, choosing his words carefully to skirt the narrow line between the truth and a lie, "I know all about Slick Pratt and his men. Blaze, Clem, and Fred, ain't that their names?" He watched Mae's face change from sullenness to fear. "And I know a lot more that I'm not telling you just yet. But I figured I owed you something because we did have a good time in Gallup, so I thought I'd give you a chance to talk first."

"About what?"

"About who's really behind this scheme to get the Hopis and the Navajos fighting so the government can take back the land it gave 'em for their reservations."

"I don't know what you're talking about," Mae protested.

"Sure you do, Mae. And telling me everything you know just might save that pretty neck of yours from stretching in a hangman's noose. You study on it and I'll come back tomorrow to talk to you again."

When Mae did not reply, Longarm turned to leave. He was almost to the end of the cellblock when she called his name. He walked back down to the corridor to her cell. "It didn't take you long to change your mind," he said.

"I haven't changed my mind, Longarm. Not yet. But don't come back tomorrow. That's too soon. Make it about three days. I need some time to think about things."

"I'll think about it, too," Longarm said. "You ain't the only one that can change your mind. You remember that, Mae. But if I don't change my mind, I might come back in three days."

As he walked slowly to the jail's front door, Longarm hoped that Mae would call him back a second time, but she did not. He crossed the street to the saloon and told the jailer, "Thanks for the use of your jail. You can have it back now."

"You a friend of that Blaisdell lady?" the jailer asked.

Longarm said carefully, "I only met her once before. Why?"

"Because she don't seem to have no friends." The jailer drained his glass. "I feel sorta sorry for her. Just one visitor since she's been locked up, and he sure wasn't no friend of hers."

"Mind telling me who that visitor was?"

"Armbruster, from the Indian Bureau office. I heard part of what he told her. He said she was using reservation land, and if she was going to be locked up a long time, the Bureau might have to take it away from her. Now that wasn't friendly, was it?"

"No, I don't guess you could call it that. But I'll tell you something. The government don't have many friends."

"I guess you're right. Well, any time you wanta rent the jail, Marshal, I'll be glad to oblige."

Ignoring the dry coating of dust that lined his throat, Longarm was about to follow the jailer out of the saloon when he saw the familiar face of Tom Moore smiling at him from the label of a dust-filmed bottle on the backbar. Longarm remembered what he'd discovered in Gallup, that the Harvey Houses were temperance hotels, and that he'd be in Winslow at least three more days.

Stepping over the long mahogany, he asked the barkeep, "Is that a fresh bottle of Tom Moore I'm looking at?"

"You couldn't call it fresh, mister. That damn bottle's done nothing but gather dust for five years. Folks in Arizona Territory just don't drink rye whiskey."

"How'd you feel if I took it off your hands?"

"Mister, if you'll get that bottle outa the way so I can put something I can sell in place of it, I'll sell it to you for just what it cost me. That's one dollar."

"You got yourself a deal."

While the barkeep wiped the dust off the bottle of Maryland rye, Longarm dug a cartwheel out of his pocket and placed it on the bar. He tucked the bottle into his saddlebag and rode over to the Indian Bureau office.

Armbruster's office door stood open, but he was not at his desk. Longarm went to the adjoining office, where he found the clerk who'd prepared his vouchers.

"You look for Mr. Armbruster to be back right soon?" he asked.

"Not till the day after tomorrow, Marshal Long," the clerk said. "If you wanted to tell him you've found out about those snake-poison killings, he already knows that. But I guess you'd know he knows, because it was you who sent Mrs. Blaisdell down here to jail." The clerk shook his head. "A pity. Her husband worked for the Bureau before he died, you know."

"So I heard. You're sure Armbruster won't be back until the day after tomorrow?"

"Sure as can be. He had to go to Albuquerque on personal business. At least that's what it said in the note he left me." The clerk opened his desk drawer and took out a sheet torn from a small notepad. "Here, see for yourself." He handed the note to Longarm.

Longarm recognized the handwriting at a glance. The last sample of it he'd seen had been on the bloodstained paper from Slick Pratt's pocket. He also realized that the three days asked for by Mae Blaisdell would cover the day following the bureau chief's return from his personal business trip to Albuquerque, where he could send telegrams without using his real name.

"If that's the case, then, I'll go on over to the Harvey House and check in and wait till he gets back," Longarm told the clerk. "I'll drop in on him then. The business I got with him can wait." As he turned away, Longarm muttered, "Only I wouldn't like to have it wait too long."

Chapter 20

"Really, Longarm, I don't see how you could possibly have been as pleased as you seemed to be when I arrived this afternoon," Becky Cranborn said. "I must have looked— no, I'm absolutely positive that I did look a fright after that terrible trip down here from Black Mesa. And you—why, you looked as though you'd just stepped from a bandbox!"

"That sure wasn't how I looked the day I got back," Longarm smiled. "I looked worse'n you did. The Harvey Houses has got a newfangled way to fix up folks' travelling clothes while they're sleeping at night. That's how come I look halfway decent today."

"Luckily I had fresh clothing waiting for me in my trunk," Becky said. "And a hot bath in a real tub, then a nap, has made me feel like a new person."

"You look like one, too," Longarm said. "A real pretty lady, Becky, not like a professor at all."

Indeed, there was little resemblance between the Professor Cranborn whom Longarm had met on Black Mesa and the Becky Cranborn he was now looking at with open admiration as they sat having after-dinner coffee in the Harvey House dining room.

Professor Cranborn had been tall and angular, a dowdy woman, her hair pulled back in a no-nonsense hairdo, who had worn a suit of cotton duck, a split skirt with a loose, shapeless jacket, and heavy outdoor brogans. Becky looked ten years younger in her present guise than when she wore her working garb. Her silver-blonde hair was puffed into a soft haloed roll around her head. She had on a dress with a bouffant skirt. The dress did not disguise her height, but made it less apparent, and certainly did not disguise the generous cleavage its low-cut bodice revealed.

Becky said, "On Black Mesa I was a professor, Longarm. Now I'm a British gentlewoman. In that arroyo, I was—well, truthfully, I was just frightened. But that seems a long time ago."

"Yes, I reckon it does," Longarm agreed.

"I like the food here better than in either place. In fact all I need now—" She stopped short.

"Go on," Longarm urged. "If you'll tell me what you're hankering for, I'll sure order it up."

"Well, I usually have a brandy with my coffee after dinner."

"That's one thing we can't get in the Harvey House, Becky. They're all temperance hotels."

"Oh, dear! I've learned what that means in America. Isn't there somewhere we could go for a coffee and brandy?"

"There's saloons, but they don't serve ladies like you."

"I shall resign myself to going without, then."

Longarm hesitated for a moment, then said, "Now, if you'd really like a drink and don't mind going into a man's hotel room, I've got a bottle upstairs. It ain't brandy, it's Maryland rye whiskey, but it's what I favor."

"Really? A whiskey made of rye grains? How quaintly American." Becky looked at him thoughtfully. "Yes, Longarm, I think I'd like to taste your Maryland rye whiskey, and it doesn't embarrass me to visit a man in his hotel room. After all, when one's travelling, a hotel room is one's flat—one's castle."

In his room, Longarm poured each of them a generous tot of Tom Moore. Lighting a cheroot, he raised his glass in a salute and swallowed the rye in a gulp. Becky sipped hers at first, then followed his example and drained her glass. He watched her face for a reaction, but all he saw was a slight flicker of her eyelids as the sharp-smooth rye went down her throat.

"Well?" Longarm asked. "What do you think of it?"

"Interesting, Longarm. Very interesting indeed. Quite

177

pungent, yet it has a bouquet which I imagine grows on one."

"It does." Longarm was suddenly aware that Becky was watching him intently. He asked, "Something wrong, Becky?"

"Of course not. I was just thinking how different this is from being tied up, wondering what was going to happen to us."

"It's a lot better, all right. Of course, I don't guess anybody really knows what's going to happen to 'em next."

"You and I do, Longarm. At least in the immediate future."

"Meaning you'll be going back to England, and I'll—"

"I wasn't thinking that far ahead," Becky broke in. "I meant tonight. I know exactly what's going to happen."

"I'd be right interested in hearing what it is."

"As soon as you realize that I had in mind the same thing you did when you invited me up here to try your rye whiskey, we're going to be in that bed over there."

"That's straight enough talk to suit anybody," Longarm smiled. "You English ladies don't make no bones about saying what you've got in mind," He started to take off his coat. "And I'll talk straight as you do. Ever since you came into the dining room with that low-cut dress pushing them pretty white tits up at me, I've been wondering what you'd look like with it off."

"My dear Longarm, you won't waste time wondering." Becky stood up and started sliding the dress off her shoulders. "As it happens, I'm quite proud of my teats."

Watching the twin globes emerge as Becky slid the dress down to her waist, he said, "They're even prettier than I figured."

"Shall I tell you now what I've been wondering about you?"

"I don't guess you need to, but go ahead anyhow."

"Ever since I helped you wet that rawhide in the arroyo, I've been wondering how big that magnificent member of yours is when it's hard, and how it'll feel inside me."

Becky stepped out of her low-heeled pumps. Longarm

178

kept his eyes on her while he took off his gunbelt, crossed the room, and hung it on the bedpost. He sat on the bed to lever his boots off and started unbuttoning his shirt. Becky let her dress fall to the floor and came over to the bed. She wore only a pair of thin white silk knickers, and Longarm saw the golden glint of soft pubic curls gleaming in the vee of her thighs.

"Would you like to take off the final fig leaf?" she asked.

"It'll be my pleasure."

Longarm looked at the rose-pink nipples that were level with his eyes, leaned forward and nibbled the tips gently with his lips, one and then the other, while his hands brushed down her hips and slid the knickers down her thighs. His face was buried in the soft perfumed crease between the snowy hemispheres of her breasts when he felt Becky's fingers on his fly.

He stood up, and after he'd gotten over the surprised realization that she stood almost as tall as he did, ran a line of kisses up her neck and across her chin until their lips met. Becky's lips parted and Longarm thrust his tongue in to meet hers. She had pushed his trousers and balbriggans down to his knees now, and her hands were fingering his shaft.

Suddenly she broke their kiss and asked softly, "Longarm, would you be shocked if I told you that when I had this big beautiful thing in my hands in the arroyo, just a few inches from my mouth, I had a sudden mad urge to gulp it in?"

"Maybe I wouldn't've been shocked, but I'd sure have been surprised if you'd done it, the fix we was in."

"We're not in any trouble now, and I've got the same urge."

"Then I guess we better do something about it."

Longarm lifted Becky to the bed. Still holding on to his shaft, she sank down on her back and when Longarm kneeled beside her, began running her hot wet tongue back and forth along its hard pulsing length. Longarm waited until she obeyed her urge and engulfed him with her mouth, then turned to straddle her head so that she could reach him more easily. He rolled the tips of her breasts between his fingertips and in response Becky's hips jerked convulsively. Her hands were moving over his crotch, fondling him, while her lips kept pulling at his erection.

Longarm looked at the supple length of Becky's milk-white body stretched on the bed below him. Her hips were twisting from side to side, her knees raised and her thighs parted. The eager rasping of her tongue over his sensitive flesh and the golden glint of her soft pubic curls invited him to share with her the pleasure he was beginning to feel.

Lowering himself gently, Longarm spread Becky's thighs still wider. Framed by the fleece of gold, her saw her second lips, a richer, warmer pink than the tips of her breasts, and dropped his head to find them with his tongue. He found the sensitive button he was seeking and caressed it with quick flicks of his tongue-tip. Becky brought up her hips, and Longarm took the button between his lips, nibbling it as he'd nibbled on her breasts.

Becky released him suddenly and said, "No, Longarm! No more right now! I can't hold back much longer, and I want you in me deep when I let go!"

Longarm shifted his position quickly. He swung around and kneeled between Becky's legs. She grabbed his shaft and guided him in. Longarm sank into her hot, wet depths with a long, slow thrust. Becky reared up to meet him and locked her legs around his waist, letting him lift her hips as he raised his. Then, to prolong her pleasure at his deep penetration, she relaxed her grip and dropped away as he thrust down, rising to meet him only as he neared the finish of each long, deep stroke.

He'd been pounding into her for only a few moments when Becky gasped, "I thought I could hold on longer, but I can't! Don't stop, Longarm, even if I tell you to!"

"Don't worry. I ain't anywheres near ready, yet."

A little scream escaped from Becky's throat. She grasped Longarm's head and pulled it down until their lips met. Her hot tongue darted into his mouth. She began shivering, rolling her hips wildly. Longarm kept pounding steadily while she tossed and gasped and then subsided into a series of rippling quivers. After a few moments her tense muscles relaxed and she lay inert.

Longarm did not stop, but continued stroking at a slower pace until Becky's languor passed and she began to respond again.

"You must be almost ready, Longarm," she whispered. "Will you come with me now?"

"I sure as hell will. But next time I'll hold out longer."

Becky's hips were soon gyrating furiously again, and Longarm was responding, too. He paced his stroking until the moans of Becky's approaching spasm rose to a fevered pitch, then pounded faster as he passed the point where he could hold control.

To the accompaniment of her cries he thrust deeply into Becky's quivering nest and their bodies shook together as Longarm came to his own climax. He held himself locked against her while he let go, joining Becky in a long, shuddering release until their muscles went slack and they lay limp and exhausted.

"My word, Longarm, you're incredible," Becky whispered when he made no move to leave her. "I thought you were pulling my leg when you said there'd be a next time, but your marvelous member's just as big and hard as ever."

"There'll be a next time," Longarm promised. "And another time after that, unless you get too tired."

Becky's sigh of pleasure started deep in her throat and gusted into Longarm's ear. "I'll never be too tired for what you're giving me. Start whenever you're ready, Longarm. My train doesn't leave until late tomorrow night."

Longarm woke instantly and sat up in the bed, his hand going instinctively to the butt of the Colt that hung in his gunbelt on the headboard. He looked toward the door, but it was not in its usual place. Then he realized that he was not in his familiar room in Denver, but still in the Harvey House in Winslow. Reaching for his vest on the chair beside the bed, he fished out his watch and was surprised when he saw the hands aligned at twelve.

You got to get cracking, old son, he told himself. Rolling off the bed, Longarm padded to the bureau where the half-empty bottle of Tom Moore stood waiting, tilted the bottle, and let a stream of pungent rye trickle down his throat. *But that lady professor wasn't about to let you stop till she'd tried all the ways she wanted to go at it. If it wasn't for having to catch her train, she'd still be here ready for another next time, but she's gone now, and you got to get to work.*

Carrying the bottle with him, Longarm went back and sat on the bed. Dismissing the pleasant memories of his time with Becky Cranborn, he lighted a cheroot and took another swallow of the whiskey. Then, while he dressed, he concentrated on reviewing the facts he'd dug out.

What you got, old son, Longarm concluded, *is a lot of loose ends that don't mean diddledy-squat till you've pulled 'em all together into a nice, neat knot. And by the time you've had some breakfast and a shave, that westbound Santa Fe train will just about be pulling in, and you'll have hold of the last little bitty string you need to tie that knot.*

Longarm was waiting at the depot when the Santa Fe's westbound train chugged to a stop and the passengers began to get off. Tom Armbruster was among the last to alight. A surprised frown flitted across his face, but the Indian Bureau chief was smiling when he stopped in front of Longarm.

"I thought you'd be on your way back to Denver by now, Marshal Long," Armbruster said. "I hope I didn't delay you by being out of town when you solved your case."

"That didn't bother me one bit," Longarm replied. "I had to talk to Mae Blaisdell before I could pull out of town."

Armbruster looked at the people moving around on the station platform and said, "I've got to get to the Bureau office now that I'm back. Suppose you walk along there with me, and we can talk on the way." As they began walking, he went on, "Mae was the last person I'd have suspected of committing those murders. I went to the jail and talked to her after Tosih Nez brought her in. Of course, I was just following Bureau rules. I had to warn her that we'd have to revoke her permit if she was found guilty."

"I guess all of us who work for Uncle Sam have got rules. I needed to get her to write out a confession and sign it so's there'd be some evidence to take to court."

"I hope you got what you were after. It didn't occur to

182

me that you'd want her to sign a confession. Did she?"

"She ain't yet. Fact is, she won't say a word to me. But I ain't giving up. I'll be talking to her again, today or tomorrow, and maybe I can get her to change her mind."

They'd reached the Indian Bureau building, and Armbruster said, "Since you were waiting for me at the depot, I suppose you need something from the Bureau before you start back. If your expense voucher didn't cover what you were out of pocket, I can have the clerk take care of that right now."

"That can wait a while. I got something else on my mind that I want to go over with you," Longarm replied.

"Come in then, Marshal. I'll be glad to help you any way I can."

Longarm followed Armbruster into his office. The bureau chief placed his satchel in a corner and settled down behind his desk. He went on, "Now, then, what do you need?"

"I didn't have a chance to mention till now that I had a brush with Slick Pratt and his men up on Black Mesa, where they was holding a horse herd to turn loose," Longarm said.

Armbruster stared across the desk, frowning. "Am I supposed to know who Slick Pratt is, Marshal? I don't recall having heard the name before."

"Well, that's right funny, now. I took a note off Slick's body after he was shot that says some friends of yours back in New York were going to give him a thousand dollars when he'd got the Navajos and Hopis to fighting so the Indian Bureau'd be put back in charge of their reservations."

"Hold on, Marshal. You couldn't have seen my name signed to something as ridiculous as that."

"Your name wasn't signed to it, Armbruster. You were too smart to sign it. But that note was in your handwriting, and it wouldn't take but one look for a judge and a jury to tell who wrote it. Hell, I came in here right after I got back to Winslow and your clerk showed me a note you'd written him. It didn't take me any time to tell that you wrote the note to Slick Pratt, too."

"Show me the note to this man Pratt, Marshal!" Armbruster demanded. "You owe me a chance to prove you're wrong!"

Longarm shook his head. "Even if I had the note on me, which I don't right now, I wouldn't give you a chance to tear it up. You sent Slick Pratt and his gang up there to get the Navajos and Hopis so riled up over their grazing rights that they'd start a war, so the Indian Bureau could take over from their tribal councils and run the reservations again. Didn't you? And you got Mae Blaisdell to kill those four men by threatening the two things that meant the most to her—her livelihood, since you could revoke her permit for running the trading post; and her daughter, who you'd somehow found out about and were threatening to harm.

"You figured that the Navajos would blame the Hopis for the deaths of those two Navajo elders, since the Hopis are known to be friendly with the rattlesnakes. And what about Jack Foster? Did he find out something about your little scheme, or was he on Mae's tail for the first two killings? Either way, you got rid of him, too, and that other Navajo, Soshei Toh. I saw Soshei Toh's body, Armbruster. That was one hell of a way to die."

Armbruster's panic had subsided. He sat silently for a moment, his nervousness betrayed only by his hands, which kept toying with the inkwell that stood on his desk.

Longarm decided to push. His voice cold, he said, "You're like a lot of crooked schemers, Armbruster. You think nobody is as smart as you are. Don't you think I know why you wanted the Indian Bureau back in charge of the Navajo and Hopi land?"

"I don't think you can prove I had any reason to get involved in a scheme that would mean an Indian war, Long. I've got a good job here. Why risk it?"

"Money," Longarm snapped. "Big money—mining that coal from Black Mesa. If some big outfit from New York came in here to start mining, they'd have to pay a pretty big chunk of money for mineral rights to the Hopis and the Navajos, wouldn't they?"

"Of course. But your case doesn't hold up, Long. Under Indian Bureau rules they'd have to pay the Indians anyhow."

"But if you were the Indian Bureau chief that set the price, they'd save enough to give you a right big cut of their profit. And what it'd take to buy up people like Mae Blaisdell and Slick Pratt would be small change. Oh, I got a case all right, and I bet when I look in that satchel you took to Albuquerque I'll find all I need to prove it!"

"Damn you, Long!" Armbruster exploded.

He had in his hands the inkwell he'd been toying with. He flung it across the desk at Longarm. The top snapped open and a flood of blue ink splashed into Longarm's face. Blinded momentarily, his eyes stinging, Longarm blinked quickly enough to see Armbruster yank the drawer of the desk open, and through the blue haze saw the bureaucrat's hand grab a pistol from the drawer.

At that close range, Longarm did not need his Colt. He slid his derringer from his vest pocket and fired across the desk. Armbruster slumped. The pistol he held dropped back into the drawer from his nerveless fingers, and he crumpled to the floor.

Longarm looked up from Armbruster's lifeless body and caught sight of his blue-streaked face reflected in the pane of the window behind the desk.

"You better find a washbowl quick, old son, before that ink sinks in," he said aloud. "If you go out on the street, Tosih Nez or one of them other Navajo policemen is liable to run you in on a charge of being a Navajo on the warpath!"

Watch for

LONGARM ON THE GREAT DIVIDE

fifty second novel in the bold LONGARM series
from Jove

coming in February!